**She'd won the trip of her dreams, but she'd had no idea what she was really getting into...**

After several hours of questioning, they allowed Fiona to return to her compartment. The police had warned her that she could not leave the train when it arrived at Istanbul other than to accompany them to the local station.

She almost vomited when they said that. Even though she knew she was innocent, she was terrified that they would blame her anyway. It would be easy for them to do since there was that unexplained letter calling her a Mata Hari and all the unrest on the continent that already existed.

She knew if they did a cursory investigation into her family, they'd find out about her father's fascist tendencies. Never mind that she'd moved out due to his politics, it would be assumed that she believed the same as he did. She never would have believed such a thing could be happening to her.

In her cabin, she tugged off her perky little hat from the morning that looked as wilted and sad as she felt now. She still could scarcely take in the situation in which she found herself. A murder suspect of all things. Last week she was at work amongst all the books she loved, and now, here she was all the way almost to the easternmost edge of the continent basically all alone and at the mercy of foreign police. So much for being excited about winning a contest for a trip to Istanbul.

**Her dreams of a trip across Europe on a luxury train hadn't included murder...**

In 1937, with the clouds of war looming on the horizon, librarian Fiona Vancleave dreams of luxury train trips involving exotic places and romantic interludes. But when she wins a trip on the *Orient Express*, she quickly discovers that things aren't quite as she envisioned them. While romance might be a possibility with fellow passenger, the enigmatic Winchester Barrington, IV, Fiona doesn't know if she can trust him, especially when she finds herself suspected of murder. Alone in a foreign country, facing possible jail time or even execution is certainly not what she had in mind when she booked her trip.

**He's a spy, searching for an assassin, but he hadn't expected to find romance...**

Winchester Barrington, IV, scion of a wealthy Connecticut family, boards the Orient Express, ostensibly for a pleasure trip from Paris to Istanbul. In reality, he's a spy for the United States War Department on the trail of a master assassin. His mission: to find and capture this elusive executioner. Among a growing list of suspects, including an Oxford Don, an American entrepreneur, a Chicago gangster, and two mysterious Turkish men, Win finds himself attracted to Fiona, a shy librarian who may actually be his quarry.

# KUDOS for *Senior Assassin*

In *Senior Assassin* by Sherry Fowler Chancellor, Fiona Vancleave wins a trip on the *Orient Express* in 1937. An English librarian, Fiona is thrilled to win this luxury trip from Paris to Istanbul. On board the train, she meets Winchester Barrington, IV, who is undercover for the US War Department, looking for a super spy. Because Fiona is shy and has a German-sounding last name, and because Germany is on the verge of war, Fiona becomes the main suspect when people start dying. The storyline is intriguing, the characters charming, and the romance sweet. Chancellor gives an authentic view of what life was like for a "middle class" librarian, trying to mingle with "upper class" aristocrats on a luxury train. If you're looking for something an old-fashioned mystery/romance, it would be hard to go wrong with *Senior Assassin*. – *Taylor Jones, Reviewer*

*Senior Assassin* by Sherry Fowler Chancellor is an old-fashioned, Agatha Christie-type mystery. I guess today you would call this a cozy mystery. Since I'm a big Agatha Christie fan, this book was right up my alley. It's a refreshing change from all the blood and gore so prevalent in mysteries today. That's not to say there's no blood in the book, but Chancellor does keep it to a minimum. The plot is strong, the characters charming and well-developed, and romance sweet and heartwarming. This is the kind of book you'll want to keep on your shelf to read over and over again. – *Regan Murphy, Reviewer*

# ACKNOWLEDGEMENTS

I couldn't have written this book without the assistance of E. H. Cookridge who wrote the definitive book on the Orient Express called *Orient Express: The Life and Times of the World's most Famous Train.* It was an invaluable resource for me. Although I never spoke to the author, his work was my go-to book for the history of this beautiful train.

I also want to acknowledge the contributions of my father, Donald Fowler, who has actually ridden the train – his memories of the interior, as well as the journey, assisted me in imaging my characters and their environment.

I did take a few liberties with the speed of the journey in order to move the plot along. Forgive me for that intentional error.

# Senior

# Assassin

Sherry Fowler Chancellor

*A Black Opal Books Publication*

GENRE: HISTORICAL ROMANCE/ROMANTIC SUSPENSE/MYSTERY
-DETECTIVE

SENIOR ASSASSIN
Copyright © 2014 by Sherry Fowler Chancellor
Cover Design by Sherry Fowler Chancellor
All cover art copyright © 2014
All Rights Reserved
Print ISBN: 978-1-626941-80-9

First Publication: SEPTEMBER 2014

Published by Black Opal Books **http://www.blackopalbooks.com**

# DEDICATION

*To my son, Rhett Chancellor*
*my Parisian traveling companion and*
*the one who inspired the title of this story.*

# Chapter 1

For secrets are edged tools, and must be kept
from children and from fools. ~ *John Dryden,*
*English poet, 1631-1700*

*Paris, France, 1937*:

The station platforms at Gare de l'Est Paris were crowded with people off to various destinations. The sea of humanity made for lots of noise and bustle. Porters followed behind travelers and carried their bags and steamer trunks to be loaded onto eight different trains. Early morning fog seeped into the area from the openings leading out from the rail yard to the tracks. It was a cool day and passengers in heavy coats hustled toward the warmth of the cars. Steam hissed from the engine of the train on track number two and seemed to ooze from beneath it as well. Covered in a cloud of fog and steam, Winchester Barrington, IV looked down at his sister, Cordelia. "You better get on board before you get soot all over that new coat."

She glanced down at the ankle-length fine-wool coat with a fur collar and smiled. "This old thing?"

"Yeah. *That* old thing." He ran his index finger across the fur. "You've had it, what? A week?"

"Never mind about the age of my garment. What are you going to do after I board?"

"I'm scoping out the other passengers."

"Wouldn't it be better for me to stand here then so you don't seem obvious?"

"No. Remember, I'm trained for this. I know how to look casual." He tilted his head to indicate the locomotive. "Go on now. Board the train and get yourself some tea or coffee."

"I still think this is a little incestuous, Barry. I don't like it." Cordelia frowned.

"It would only be incestuous, dear little sister, if we were going to actually bunk down together."

"But the cabin steward will make the bed into a double since we're 'married.' You know that."

Barry grasped Cordelia's upper arm. "I plan to tell him that you're pregnant and on doctor's orders to sleep alone."

She swung her hand to smack him but he caught her wrist just short of her making contact. "Do *not* make a scene, Cordelia. Don't. I need you on this mission but if I have to, I'll leave you right here." He leaned in to where his nose was almost touching hers. "Got it?"

"I have it, you monster, but we're going to talk about this. I will *not* be pregnant. You'll have to think of something else. I don't care a tinker's damn about your mission. You're not going to bandy that rumor around on this train."

"You're *not* to use this trip to try to pick up men either. You can't be your normal flirtatious self. You agreed to this plan, if I'd get you out of the house and away from mother's constant chaperoning, so you better cooperate. Now get on the train." He was tempted to throttle her but he'd been raised better than that. Nonetheless, the thought did cross his mind.

Cordelia let out a huge puff of air that made the fur on her coat flutter but she obeyed his command.

Once she was off the platform, Win concentrated on the other passengers as they boarded. He held a leather portfolio and took notes in such a manner as if to appear to be studying the station and jotting information for further reflection. It was a good cover in his opinion. He was pretending to be an engineer. Well, not really *pretending* since he had a degree in it but that wasn't really his job.

He noticed a few couples, several single male travelers and one lone woman clutching a wicker bag that reminded him of a fisherman's creel. She held it tight to her chest as if she feared someone would steal it. She glanced around as if in awe.

She was blonde and a bit short for his taste. She had on a black coat and the skirt peeking out from the bottom was also black. Her hair was tied up in a severe bun as if she hated the thought of being perceived as feminine. In fact, it was scraped back so tightly, she must have had a headache.

Win puzzled over her. Could she be the person he sought? Was she trying so hard to be inconspicuous that she stood out? He shook his head. No. It couldn't be. Besides, could a woman be as dangerous as he'd been led to believe his prey was? He'd read the dossier, after all. No. Not a woman and definitely not this one. She seemed too meek. He turned away and focused his attention on the others still in the process of boarding.

Two men caught his attention. One had the look of Peter Lorre about him. That fact in and of itself was enough to make him suspicious. The other one was so non-descript, Win made a note to engage him in conversation to see what he did for a living. He bet the man was a Fuller Brush salesman. He laughed under his breath. His father was friends with Alfred Fuller and he knew the man well.

The sound of "All aboard" being called by the conductor snapped Win to attention and with one last glance around the crowded, noisy, steamed-filled station, he stepped onto the bottom iron step that led on to the train. He held on to the rail, stared out past the shoeshine boys, and watched as a man in a trench coat carrying a duffle bag dashed past the other boarding areas. He was headed right toward where Win stood.

Win moved aside as the man leapt onto the now-moving train.

"Thanks, mate. Bugger that fog. My cab hit the car in front of us and I had to run the rest of the way." The man swept off his hat and placed his bag on the floor. He held his hand out. "Mack Plant. Nice to meet you."

"Winchester Barrington, IV. My friends call me Barry."

Plant grabbed Win's hand and shook it. "Barry it is, then."

The conductor approached. "May I show you gentlemen to your quarters?"

Plant held out his ticket. "Indeed, dear chap. Thank you so much."

The conductor glanced down at it. "Ahh. Yes, sir. You're near the back." He held out his hand for Win's. "And you, sir, are near the dining car." He pointed to his left. "That way. It's the second door before you get to the dining car. You can make your way there or wait for me to come back from escorting this gentleman."

"I can find it. Thanks." Win turned toward the front of the train.

As the conductor led Plant away, the man called over

his shoulder, "Would love to chat with you in the club car later, mate."

"That would be nice," Win replied. He walked on toward his cabin, mulling over what was not quite right about the man called Mack Plant. Was it his ludicrous name or was it the slightly trying too hard to be British accent and syntax?

As Win moved down the corridor, his mind turned to Cordelia and he wondered yet again if involving his sister in this plan was going to pan out to be the biggest mistake of his life. He couldn't afford to let down his commander and his gut was warning him that he might do just that.

෬෨෬

The cacophony of noise in the station overwhelmed Fiona Vancleave as she clutched her basket to her chest. It was all she could do not to cover her ears as she boarded the train. She'd been on trains before but mostly from her home in Worchester, England and there was usually only one at the station at any time, since there were only two platforms there.

The noise of the eight different platforms was overwhelming. There seemed to be people everywhere, with everyone seeming to know where they headed.

Excited to be on an adventure, the twenty-three-year-old librarian couldn't settle her heart rate down as she watched all the activity.

The hustle and bustle of the porters and the other passengers gave her a thrill and once she was in her compartment, she sat and gazed out the window, transfixed by the scene.

She knew she looked like a country rube to the others in the sophisticated city of Paris but she was too thrilled to be there to worry about it.

It was her lucky day when she won the contest that allowed her to take this luxury trip across the continent. She could barely believe the day was finally here. What an adventure she was in for—or at least she hoped she was in for one.

A knock at the door pulled her from her reverie. She moved away from the window but before she could touch the knob, a steward poked his head in. "Good day, mademoiselle. I am Lucien. I will be serving as your cabin steward. Would you like me to unpack your cases?"

"No, that won't be necessary. I can do it myself."

The man bowed. "It is part of the service."

"I really don't mind doing it myself." She was really a bit put off by the thought of a man plundering through her unmentionables. No way was she letting him unpack her stuff.

"If you insist." He backed out. "Place your bags in the corridor when you're finished and I'll take them to the luggage hold."

"Thank you, Lucien."

He left and Fiona returned to her seat to watch the

action until the train moved. It didn't seem as if the stream of passengers was ever going to end.

With a large exhale of steam from the front of the train and a couple of blasts of the horn, the locomotive began to creep forward and out of the station. The huge monstrosity lumbered slowly until it was out of the rail yard, the city center, and into the relatively open area of the suburbs. Fiona sat, still watching out the window through this process, then shook herself back to attention.

Resolved to get unpacked before the steward came back and insisted on doing the job, she stood, pulled her suitcase off the rack above her head, and set it on the seat. She opened it and took out the two items on top. Before she left home in Worchester, Fiona and her best friend went shopping for a couple of formal dresses for her to wear on the trip. They were expensive but she needed to fit in with the others on the train so she'd spent the money.

The one in pale blue silk was her favorite. Fiona ran her hand down the soft material and thought about how it looked on her. It clung in all the right places and made her forget she was a librarian. It wasn't often that she could play the part of a femme fatale but she planned to try on this six-day trip across the continent. It was probably the only chance she'd get in this lifetime, since she didn't travel first class as a rule.

Making quick work of the other unpacking after she'd hung up her other evening gown, Fiona pulled her hair out of the severe bun she'd fixed that morning and combed it. She wanted to go to the lounge and get a drink and was determined to try to look less studious than she did each day at work. She found a thick barrette and pulled her hair back in it. Curls hung down her back and she tugged a few tendrils loose around her face to soften her appearance.

Satisfied, she zipped her suitcase closed and remembering what Lucien said, she opened the door and set it out in the corridor. After pocketing her key, Fiona walked past her case and down the hall toward the direction the conductor had told her was the way to public cars that included the lounge and the dining area.

She moved down the corridor swaying a little in motion with the train. She'd never been much good at keeping her balance on a moving vehicle and this time was no different.

Jostling along and hitting her hip on the wall periodically made Fiona giggle.

When the train took a curve, she really lost her balance and fell into a man walking behind her. "I'm so sorry. I can't walk very well yet."

"It's all right, mademoiselle. It's kind of like trying to find your sea legs on a ship, isn't it?" The man removed his hand from her waist. He smelled like peppermints. "I hope you're steadier now. Are you going to the lounge?"

"Yes. I am thank you."

"Then allow me to escort you there. I'm Jacques Cassel." The man was of average height and build, and he wore his medium brown hair a little long. He seemed as if he'd blend into a crowd easily and his manner was mild and pleasant.

Fiona smiled. "That would be lovely. Maybe I can stay on my feet between here and there."

His lips curved into a grin that seemed a bit more menacing than friendly. "If not, I'm here to assist."

Fiona shrugged off the unease his facial expression caused her and moved down to the lounge car with him. She sensed she was already in over her head and they weren't even completely out of the Paris city limits yet. What made her think she was any match for the rich and idle? It seemed to her as if this man had already figured out that she was a mousy, poor librarian from the country and he was ready to devour her for dinner.

Her steward passed them and nodded his head at her. "Mademoiselle, may I collect your baggage now?"

"Yes, Lucien, that would be lovely. I left it out for you."

She continued down the corridor with Monsieur Cassel behind her.

His peppermint scent wafted over her. When they arrived at the lounge, he opened the door and stepped aside. As she passed him on her way inside, he said, "May I know the name of the lovely lady I accompanied?"

"Fiona. I'm Fiona Vancleave."

"I shall remember that, my dear, and hope to see you again and again as we travel to Istanbul."

"I'm sure you will since this is really a small world in itself."

"Perhaps dinner, then, some evening. I'd enjoy a drink with you now but am meeting a friend." Cassel reached for her hand and lifted it to his lips. He placed a kiss on her knuckles. "For now, *au revoir*."

When he let go of her hand, it was all she could do not to wipe it on her skirt. She couldn't figure out why he gave her the jitters but he did and she didn't like it.

# Chapter 2

In skating over thin ice, our safety is in our speed. ~ *Ralph Waldo Emerson, American Writer1803-1882*

Fiona stopped right inside the door, overwhelmed by the décor of the lounge car. She could scarcely believe she was on a train. She hoped her mouth was shut and she didn't look like the girl from the country that she was. The lounge chairs and benches had red velvet cushions with tufted seats. The bar was polished to such a high sheen, that Fiona was sure it would act almost like an iced-over pond if a glass was placed on top and shoved down the mahogany surface. It would slip and slide all the way to the end.

There were quite a few people already seated and drinking. Some appeared to be well on the way to being drunk.

Fiona wasn't sure where she should sit since most of the tables were already taken. Both the men and women in the luxurious room intimidated her.

They were all dressed in what she knew to be expensive clothes. Self-conscious about her own wardrobe, she decided to slink over to the end of the bar and hide out over there. She really needed a gin and tonic to settle her nerves.

She entered the rest of the way into the lounge and scooted sideways along the bar behind the seats. The stool at the end had her name on it and, as she got within range of being able to sit, Fiona was interrupted by a tall, dark-haired, woman in a yellow silk dress. The frock had to cost more than her monthly salary and Fiona was even more uncomfortable about her own attire.

"Hello there. Are you traveling alone?" the woman asked.

"I am." Fiona nodded. The woman was gorgeous and Fiona was shocked that she'd taken notice of her.

The woman grabbed Fiona's upper arm. "Come sit with me and my bro—husband, I mean. I'm bored and he thinks it's tedious to put up with me."

"Your husband thinks you're tedious? How long have you been married? You look pretty young." Fiona wanted to slap her hand over her mouth as soon as the words came out. Dear God, she'd just put her foot into it, hadn't she?"

"I'm twenty-three. Come on. Sit with me. I need a friend." The woman dragged Fiona over to a table in the corner where a handsome man sat with a newspaper in his hand.

The man glanced up from the paper. "What are you doing, Cordelia?"

"I'm sorry, Barry. I need someone to talk to. You're over there ignoring me and I found—what's your name, dear?—a friend. Surely you can't begrudge me a companion on this trip if you're going to be so busy."

"Cordelia, you know this was not part of the plan." His face stern, he made eye contact with Fiona. "You must forgive my wife. She's a bit high strung but she means no harm. I suggest you go on about your business as if she hadn't interrupted you. I'm sorry she bothered you." He went back to reading his paper.

Fiona, appalled by the man's lack of respect for his spouse, opened her mouth to say something, thought better of it, and bit her tongue as she turned to move back to the bar, still seeking that glass of gin.

Someone grabbed her arm. Fiona whirled around.

It was the woman, Cordelia. "Do please ignore the ogre in the corner. I'm famished for both scintillating company and some food. Please. Sit. Let's order a bite to eat and forget this man exists."

"I'm afraid he doesn't like me."

"Pshaw. Barry doesn't like anyone. Ignore him." Cordelia pulled out a chair for Fiona and practically placed her in it. "I'll call a waiter over. What do you want?"

"A gin and tonic please." Fiona resigned herself to sit with the effusive Cordelia and her anti-social husband. How they ever married was a mystery to her but she guessed it was some kind of thing arranged by their parents. That did still happen sometimes in the upper classes she knew.

The fact that these two were American made it more puzzling for her. But that had to be what it was since they sure didn't act like they liked each other.

"But what about food? What do you want to eat? I'm famished."

"I'm not hungry. Just the drink, please."

"Very well." Cordelia sat and waved her hand in the air. A waiter scurried over and took their order. Once he was gone, she asked, "What's your name again?"

Fiona suppressed her grin. She'd never even told the woman her name at all. "I'm Fiona Vancleave."

"And you're British of course. I can tell by your accent."

"I'm from Worchester."

The waiter was back with their drinks. Fiona grabbed hers and took a huge gulp. It went down the wrong way and she choked. She coughed and tried to catch her breath.

Cordelia reached over and banged on Fiona's back. "Are you all right?" she asked, peering into Fiona's face.

Finally recovering, Fiona smiled. "I'm fine. I drank too fast."

Cordelia's husband rattled his paper as he folded it and set it on the table. He stared at Fiona, making her nervous. "You and Cordelia are more alike than I first thought. She's always in such a hurry and can't wait for things. Since she seems to have taken a liking to you and I have a hunch that she's going to hang about with you on this trip, I certainly hope you don't have a drinking problem."

"Barry." Cordelia's voice was as cold as the ice cubes in her glass of whiskey. "Stop it. I won't have you treating my friend this way."

"How dare you call me an alcoholic. You don't even know me." Furious, Fiona tried to set her glass on the table but hit the edge instead and it fell to the floor.

"Tsk." The man shook his head, stood and walked toward the bar. "Let me get someone over her to clean up your mess."

When he was gone, Fiona turned to Cordelia. "How can you stand to be married to that prig? He's nothing like you. You seem so open and friendly and he's an awful, awful man."

"He's not really that bad. He's just a bit full of himself. He always has been."

"So you've known him a long time?"

"My whole life."

"Wow. That's really something."

"What?" Cordelia took a sip of her drink.

"That you married someone you've known all your life. I can't imagine that. I want to meet a man who will sweep me off my feet. I wouldn't want to marry any of those boys I grew up with." Fiona shuddered as she thought about some of the males she played with as a child.

"To tell you the truth, I don't plan to stay married to him past this train trip." Cordelia leaned forward. "What do you think about that?"

"A divorce?" Fiona gasped. What a scandal that would be. She could scarcely believe her ears. She'd just met the woman and now she was sharing confidences that should probably be left unsaid. It must have been because she was American. Fiona had never met one but had heard others speak of how open they were about everything.

"It's not so bad." Cordelia smiled. "He'll be glad, too. But enough about me. What about you? What's your story? Why are you on your way to Istanbul? No offense, but you don't seem to be the type to gallivant across Europe." The woman reached over and patted Fiona's hand. "You know, you seem more steady, calm, and a homebody."

Fiona couldn't agree more with Cordelia's assessment.

She was glad she wasn't as flighty as this girl but it still hurt to have her point out what Fiona already knew about herself.

She sat up straighter. "I won this trip and I plan to enjoy it."

Cordelia squealed and literally bounced in her seat. "Oh, do tell. How ever did you win a trip? What fabulous prize. You're one lucky girl."

"I wrote an essay."

"Ooh, what kind? Who sponsored the contest? What did you write about?"

Fighting the urge to pinch her nose to stave off the headache Cordelia was bringing on with her incessant questions, Fiona took a deep breath before answering her. "It was an essay on train travel in the twentieth century and was sponsored by this line. They wanted people to write about the changes that had already occurred in this era and what the future holds. I don't know why they picked mine but they did. I'm supposed to give a lecture about it as well."

"That's very exciting. I can't wait. Will the lecture be here on the train itself?" Cordelia bounced again. "How did you know all that stuff to write such a thing?"

"I work in a library and—"

"Excellent. I love it. You showed the men, didn't you?" Cordelia clapped her hands. "I bet they thought a man would win. What do you do at the library?"

"I'm the assistant librarian. I've been there a couple

of years now and hope to be promoted when the current head retires."

"That's your life's goal? To be head librarian?"

"What's wrong with that?" Fiona stood to leave. There was no need for this socialite who wanted a divorce to insult *her*.

Cordelia reached out a hand and grasped Fiona's wrist. "Sorry. Sorry. Don't go. That was rude. I've been around Barry too long. Please forgive me." She glanced around. "Where is he anyway?"

Fiona looked in the same direction as Cordelia and spotted Barry chatting with the smarmy man who'd introduced himself to her earlier as Jacques Cassel. She turned back to Cordelia. "I think I want to go back to my quarters and rest."

"Nonsense. Sit back down and have another gin. Barry's tied up and I could use the company." Cordelia signaled the waiter for refills.

What chance did Fiona have against this force of nature? So she sat.

"So, Miss Librarian, what's your favorite kind of book to read?" Cordelia asked.

"Promise not to laugh?"

"I promise." Cordelia made a cross sign over her heart and smiled.

Fiona leaned in and whispered, "Spy novels. I love them."

"That's wonderful. I think that's marvelous."

"Do you really? You're not just saying that?"

"No. I truly think it's great. Tell you what, let's look around at the people here in this car and decide who's a spy. Won't that be fun?" Cordelia grabbed one of the crackers the waiter had brought with their drinks and bit into it.

"My first choice would be the one talking to your husband. He looks suspicious."

"Now you know, Fi, that the ones who look suspicious are never the ones. Spies are trained to fit in, aren't they?"

"Sure. You're right. How could I forget that?"

The waiter placed their refills on the table and Fiona picked hers up.

Cordelia inclined her head. "What about those two Turkish men over there?"

"I don't think so. I see them as two businessmen on their way home from a work trip to Paris."

"What better cover for a spy than that?"

As the words left Cordelia's mouth, her husband walked up. He glared down at her. "What the hell did you just say?"

"It's none of your business," Fiona said. "Your wife and I are having a private conversation. Who do you think you are to come over here and interrupt? I don't care if you *are* her spouse. You're the rudest man I've ever met and you treat her like she's of no importance. It's no wonder she wants a divorce."

Cordelia gasped at the same time her husband said, "I don't know why she would say such a thing to you, but she needs to quit running her mouth to strangers." He turned to Cordelia. "Come with me. I've had enough of your behavior and we are going to have a chat. Right now."

Cordelia stood. "I'm sorry, Fi. I have to go with Barry but I'll see you later."

"You don't have to put up with his abuse. I can see about moving you in with me. I'll ask the porter." Fiona didn't really want to do that since the woman's incessant chatter would wear thin quickly, but she couldn't bear to see her new friend being bossed around by the arrogant man. Who knew what he might do to her in the privacy of their car? Could he even be capable of hitting her? It sure seemed so. He was incredibly controlling.

"You'll do no such thing, Miss Vancleave. Cordelia is my responsibility." He took his wife by the arm. "Good day to you, Miss," he said as he led Cordelia away.

Fiona watched them make their way around the tables and out into the passageway. She wondered if she'd see Cordelia again or if this Barry was going to keep her locked away. They were definitely an odd match.

⌍⌎⌍

Win practically dragged Cordelia down the corridor to their compartment. Every time she opened her mouth to say something, he shushed her. Panicked at her indiscreet chat with the British woman and her bringing up spies, he was ready to throttle her even though he knew he never would. Even if she'd already blown his mission, he still loved her. She was his baby sister and, even though she could be a pain, she really didn't intend any harm. He kicked himself mentally for thinking this idea would work with her in on his secret.

When his boss had said he needed to pose as a married man, he'd suggested his sister because he didn't want to share a small train compartment with a stranger. Good Lord, he wasn't even out of France and already he was in danger of blowing the gig.

When they arrived at their compartment, Win unlocked the door and startled the steward who was unpacking their cases.

The man stepped back and bowed. "So sorry sir. I'll be right out of your way."

"That's fine." Win glanced down at the man's name-tag. "Thank you, Lucien." He handed the man a tip. "We can finish it."

Lucien picked up a small stack of garments. "I'll take these few items that need pressing with me if that's all right."

"Sure. No problem." Win wished the man would get moving. He needed to talk to Cordelia. He was ready to explode and a migraine threatened to overtake him.

Finally, the steward left, shutting the door behind

him. Win whirled around and loomed over Cordelia where she sat by the window, inspecting her manicure.

"Don't you dare act all innocent on me, Cordelia Edwina Barrington. What did you say to that woman about spies and why did you tell her you wanted a divorce? Can't you be discreet at all?"

"Oh, relax, big brother. I didn't give away the game. It seems the girl is a librarian and when I asked her what kinds of books she liked, she said spy novels. That was all we were saying. You came in snorting like a bull and whisked me out of there as if you were going to come back here and beat me with a belt. I bet that girl is calling the security forces right now."

"She better not be."

"If she is, it's your fault. You're the one who acted like a wife-beater."

"You told her you wanted a divorce."

"You bet I did. She was feeling sorry for me being shackled to you for life and I wanted to assure her that I wasn't going to be. You have to admit, you've been incredibly rude to the dear girl."

Win sat. "I don't like it. You need to retract that statement about the divorce when you see her. We're supposed to be posing as a married couple."

"I've been thinking about that. Since I already told Fiona about a possible divorce, why don't we use it to our advantage?"

Dread enveloped Win. When Cordelia had a plan, it

was always crazy and she could never be talked out of it. "How so?"

"I figure, I can be the unhappy wife and flirt a little with some of the men and maybe get some information for you that way."

"I don't think so. We need to stick to the original plan. You're merely here as window dressing. I should never have told you the amount of detail I did. This is not going to turn out well. I know it."

"It'll be fine." Cordelia patted his hand. "You'll see. Trust me. I won't let you down."

Win ran his hand over his brow. "Please stay clear and watch what you say."

Good thing he'd held back on some of the things she didn't need to know. It was bad enough he'd told her what he had.

If this thing went awry, he could lose his job or even his life, depending on how things panned out. Why, oh why had he taken this flibbertigibbet into his confidence? What an idiot he'd been.

"Nonsense, big brother, I have this under control."

Win gritted his teeth and picked up his notepad. "Can we have some quiet in here for a while? I need to make some notes."

"Fine. I'll finish unpacking since you sent away the steward." She stood and moved to the closet. "I guess you'll want some of this space for your things, too."

"Yes, dear, that's what married couples do. They share."

"Not for long, my darling husband. As soon as this journey is over, I'll be freeing myself from this yoke."

"Cordelia, please. I need to work."

"Fine. Fine." She made a lot of racket as she hung the remaining clothes and set out her toiletries in the small washroom.

Win wanted to scream but he knew she was purposely doing it to get to him. Her style had always been to annoy him in ways that he couldn't actually blame her for. He was sure if he said anything, she would blame the noise on the train moving too fast, or it taking a curve, or that his hearing was too acute, or something like that. It wouldn't be her fault in any way at all.

He inhaled a deep sigh and prayed for the strength to endure her at close quarters for the next six days.

# Chapter 3

Beware of all enterprises that require new clothes. ~ *Henry David Thoreau, American Writer, 1817-1862*

After Cordelia and her husband left the lounge, Fiona made her way toward her own compartment. She came very close to calling someone to go check on Cordelia, but finally decided that it was none of her business and she needed to stay out of the middle of their obviously unhappy marriage.

On her way, she passed a couple who coming toward her and had to fall in line in single file in order to get past. The man was tall and burly with a shock of strawberry blond hair. He wore thick-rimmed glasses and had an unlit cigar in his mouth. She was tiny and dwarfed by his size. She had her hair pulled back so tightly in a bun that it hid any wrinkles she had. It was hard to determine her age.

As they passed, the woman said something so softly that Fiona couldn't hear her. "Pardon me?" Fiona asked.

"Sorry. I said sorry." The woman smiled but it was a very shy smile and she looked away almost immediately.

"It's all right. I imagine we'll have to move aside many times in the days to come with the size of these corridors." Fiona addressed her remarks to both the man and woman.

"Forgive my wife. She's a bit soft-spoken." The man practically bellowed in an American accent.

"Nothing wrong with that," Fiona said as she edged past the couple.

"I'm Donald Perry and this is my wife, Abigail."

"Nice to meet you. I'm Fiona Vancleave." Was this train full of Americans? She'd never met one before and now here was a second couple from there.

"Vancleave, huh? Are you German? You sound like a Brit but you've got a German name."

"It's not German. It's Dutch." There was no need to tell the man about her father and his fascist tendencies that led her to move out of her parents' home.

"There's a Kleve in Germany, I think." The man persisted.

"Be that as it may, my family moved from Holland

to the United Kingdom too many years ago to count. Now, if you'll excuse me, I need to prepare for the dinner hour." Fiona moved farther down the corridor. As the couple continued their own way down the hall, she could hear the man continue to talk about how she must really be a German.

She idly wondered why the two women she'd met so far on this journey were so different from each other in personality, but they had each married a man who seemed determined to undermine them.

Was it because they were American? Did American women like to be bullied? She shook her head. She couldn't imagine that.

Maybe being a single woman wasn't so bad. Having no man to push her around and speak for her was a blessing. She'd never realized that until now.

Arriving at her door, she spied Lucien at the end of the corridor. She called out to him.

His arms full of fluffy white towels, he came to stand beside her. "Yes, mademoiselle. Is there something you needed?"

"I was wondering about assistance with dressing. Is there someone on board who could aid me with my formal gown? I realized as I was walking up the hall that I might have an issue with the top button on the back of my dress. I'm not sure I can reach it."

"Most ladies bring their own dresser with them. I can see if one of them will allow you to borrow hers for a moment. I'm afraid that all the employees on the train save one or two are male." He shrugged in a way that said he was genuinely sorry.

"Never mind. I'll manage." Fiona sniffed back the tears that threatened. Good grief, she never even thought about how she was going to get into the stupid dress when she bought it. What a ninny she'd been and now she looked like a country bumpkin to this sophisticated French man used to serving the wealthy and titled.

She opened the door to her compartment and as she stepped inside, Lucien placed a hand on the wood. "Excuse me, mademoiselle. If you wouldn't think it impertinent, I could come back and close that last button for you. There would be no need for me to ask anyone else. True, I am a man and it may not be appropriate but I have many sisters and I do not mind helping you."

Relieved that he didn't seem to be judging her, she nodded. "Thank you. That would be nice of you. Can you come around ten minutes before the dinner hour?"

"I will be here." He placed his index finger on his lips. "It will be our secret."

She entered her cabin, sat down, and burst into tears.

After her pity party, Fiona got up and washed her face at the basin in her little bathroom alcove. Determined to use this time on the train as the wonderful opportunity it was to see the world and learn about new people, she decided that she'd make an effort to engage everyone on the thing in some kind of conversation before the next two days were over. There was no reason to be ashamed of who she was. She had as much right to be on this locomotive as anyone did.

True, she may not have paid the fare herself but someone did and no one knew she couldn't afford to be here, except maybe that flighty Cordelia but she was harmless enough.

Determined to look her best, Fiona opened the closet and pulled out the blue dress. She placed it gently on the seat and turned back to the bathroom to fix her makeup and hair for the evening.

Once she was satisfied with her appearance, she slipped out of her day dress and over to the lush gown she'd been so excited to buy. It was a lovely shade of blue and hung in loose folds to the floor. The back was low, scooped out, and it hooked at the top with one large button.

Fiona struggled with the button, contorting her body in various ways to try to reach the pesky thing. She could get her hands on it but not get it through the hole, or she could grab the hole but not the button. She finally gave up and decided that she'd have to let Lucien hook it for her. She knew her mother would think it scandalous that she'd let a strange man touch her in such an intimate way but she had no choice if she didn't want to show up at dinner half-dressed.

She snorted at the thought of that. It was true that she would not be truly half-dressed but she couldn't go to the gathering with her dress unhooked. Besides, the young man said he had a passel of sisters. He didn't seem like a lecherous man. He appeared to want to be helpful.

She patted her bun, pulled out a few tendrils of hair around her face and nape to soften the look and put on some bright red lipstick. Satisfied with how she looked, she sat to wait for Lucien and think about what would be served for dinner on such a luxurious train. It certainly wouldn't be the stuff of the food trolleys on the trains at home.

She didn't have long to ponder. There was a knock at the door, which proved to be the steward. He made short work of buttoning her dress. She thanked him and he moved on down the corridor to who knew what other duties.

Fiona imagined him walking the hallways looking for damsels in distress. He sure had come to her rescue. She laughed at herself as she made her way to the dining car. She passed a couple of people on the way. She saw no one who she'd met already, although she did get a glimpse of the two Turkish men and Jacques, the man who smelled of mints.

Fiona arrived at the door to the dining room at the same time as another couple and a single man. The man was short, balding, and dressed in a very nice tuxedo. The man and woman who were together nodded at Fiona and the other gentleman and the husband opened the doors to allow the women to enter.

The dining car was even more opulent than the lounge had been, but decorated in a dark blue and gold color scheme. The seats of the chairs were shiny damask and the fabric of the curtains matched them exactly. All the crystal on the table seemed to catch the glimmer of the lights from the elaborate overhead chandeliers. It was magical and Fiona gasped in pleasure.

The wife of the couple turned to her. "It always takes my breath away, too. I never get tired of seeing it, do you?"

"It's my first time. It's gorgeous. I can hardly believe it."

"Enjoy it, my dear. There's nothing like a first trip on this special train. I'm sure I'll see you around. I'm Sarah Marchman and that's Hugo, my husband. We have a standing table that we are always assigned; but I hope to chat with you later while the men have their cigars. I look forward to hearing your impressions of your first dinner on the train." The tall, elegant woman followed her husband away from Fiona and across the room toward the far corner.

Fiona watched her leave, now worried about where she was going to sit. She didn't know they had assigned seats. In a bit of a panic, she glanced around for help.

Cordelia charged toward her with Barry in her wake. "Come, dear Fiona, and sit with us. We have a seat for you."

Happy to see a friendly face, Fiona followed along

behind them both. They sat at a table near one of the windows and, in a few moments, the short man Fiona had seen at the door joined them. He nodded at the three others. "Name's Johnny Rozzelle. Nice to meet all of you. Looks like I'm your table-mate for the journey."

Barry reached across the table. "Winchester Barrington, IV and this is my wife, Cordelia."

Rozzelle shook Barry's hand. "That's a lot of name, there, pal."

"Yeah. My friends call me Barry. A holdover from my school days."

Fiona was shocked. She'd thought his first name was Barry. Lots of men were called a shortened version of their last names but that was usually by other men. Odd that his wife would call him by that nickname. It seemed strange to her that the woman didn't use her husband's real name.

"And you are?" Rozzelle asked and peered down at her as she sat beside him.

"Oh, sorry, I'm Fiona Vancleave."

"Very nice to meet you, Fiona Vancleave." He picked up his menu. "I wonder what's on for this evening. They usually have a pretty good selection."

Fiona picked up her own menu and opened it. She was amazed at the number of choices. They must have some kind of kitchen setup to be able to offer this many options. She'd imagined that they would have one to two main dishes only.

She studied the menu and finally decided on stuffed mushrooms for her starter, prime rib for her main course, and strawberry/banana mousse for dessert. The thought crossed her mind that if she ate like that at every meal, she would soon need new clothes, but she pushed that thought away. How many first class train trips did she think were in her future anyway? Why not live it up?

Once the waiter took their orders, Cordelia turned to Johnny Rozzelle. "What do you do for a living, Mr. Rozzelle?"

"I'm into a lot of things. You could say that I'm an entrepreneur."

Cordelia leaned forward, her face eager for information. "Sounds intriguing. What kind of businesses?"

The man pulled a cigar out of his jacket pocket and ran his index finger over it. "Nothing that would interest a little miss like you."

"Please don't smoke that right now," Fiona said.

Rozzelle smiled at her as he ran the cigar under his nose. "I can if I wish. You can't stop me, little lady. Johnny does what Johnny wants."

Fiona was ready to smack the man. Who did he think he was? First he called Cordelia little miss and now he was calling her little lady? What a pig. She opened her mouth to say something but before she could, Barry's hand darted out and snatched the cigar.

Rozzelle glared. "What the hell do you think you're doing?"

"There are ladies present. You can wait and smoke when they retire to the women's lounge." Barry set the cigar down at the upper edge of Rozzelle's plate. "It'll be right there when we're finished."

"You're messing with the wrong man, Mr. Winchester Barrington, IV. I don't appreciate being treated like one of your flunkies. I don't care how much money your daddy or you have, I probably have more so you need to step away from any fight with me, young man."

"I don't care how much money anyone has, sir. Being polite when ladies are in the room is required."

Stunned at the words coming from the man who'd been nothing but rude to his own wife since the moment she'd met her, Fiona gaped at him.

The waiter stepped forward with some others behind him, each carrying a plate. In unison, they set each starter course in front of the correct passenger. When they were all served and the waiters had moved on, Rozzelle looked over at Cordelia. "I'll be keeping an eye on you."

"Did you just threaten my wife?"

"I don't think so." Rozzelle shrugged. He picked up one of his escargot, worked it free with his fork, and popped it into his mouth.

"I suggest, sir, that you request another table assignment for the duration of the trip."

"God, Barry, let's all get along. I'm sure Mr. Rozzelle doesn't mean any harm. It's all fine. Let's eat this lovely food and forget all this male posturing." Cordelia placed a hand on her husband's forearm. "Come on. Eat."

Fiona was afraid to open her mouth to say anything. Her stomach hurt and her hand shook when she picked up her fork. How she would get through the meal, she didn't know. The Rozzelle man was terrifying and she wondered if he was one of those mafia types she'd read about. He sure looked the part. She wasn't an expert by any means but he wore shiny, expensive suits and shoes and everything he'd said since he sat down made her think he might be.

The remainder of the meal passed in silence. Fiona didn't look up from her plate. She knew if she made eye contact with Cordelia that the woman would want to talk and Fiona knew she couldn't do it. She might throw up if she had to try to make chit-chat. The food was excellent but sat like lead in Fiona's stomach. When her mousse was served, she ate half of it as quickly as she could. She wiped her mouth and placed her napkin by the edge of her plate. Scraping her chair back, she stood. "Please excuse me. I need to return to my compartment."

Rozzelle stood and stepped aside to let her out. "Miss Vancleave. I hope to see you later."

She nodded as she kept her head down and made her escape.

# Chapter 4

The lie in the soul is a true lie. ~ *Benjamin Jowett, English Classicist, 1817-1893*

Once all of the women left the room, Win pulled his pipe out of the inner pocket of his dinner jacket. He took a silk tobacco pouch out of the outer pocket and opened it. He placed some in the bowl and lit it, puffing it into life. Rozzelle had moved away almost as soon as Fiona abandoned the dinner table and Win used the time it took to light his pipe to surreptitiously see where the man had gone and who he was chatting with.

It was a shame the man had to show his true colors to the ladies, but at least now Win knew the man was as dangerous as he appeared. He'd have to make sure Cordelia steered clear because this man was going on the short list of suspects.

Win wished he could take some notes but there was no way to do so yet. He'd have to hold all his observations in his head until he could escape to his compartment. For now, he needed to chat with some more of the male passengers. Even though he now knew, Rozzelle was trouble and probably up to something, he wasn't sure the older man was the one he sought for his bosses so he had to keep investigating.

Win strolled over to the large center table where a group of men had gathered. He pulled out a chair and sat down.

A waiter came over with a selection of cigars for those who weren't already smoking. The man also set down a bottle of port and some glasses. Everyone helped themselves to a snifter and one man poured his portion. He passed the bottle to the man on his left and it kept moving until all were served.

The man next to Win introduced himself as Hugo Marchman. Win recognized the name but couldn't quite place how he knew it. He didn't want to embarrass himself by asking and hoped he could pull off a conversation without making a fool of himself.

"What kind of work do you do, Barrington?" Marchman asked.

"I'm an engineer."

"Interesting. For the railway?"

"Oh, no. My family owns Barrington Industries and I work there. I'm in Europe to attend a conference and brought my wife along so she could see Paris and, of course, buy some of the latest fashions."

"Ah, yes, my wife, Lady Sarah is a big one for the Parisian fashions as well. I would bet she and your wife would hit it off."

Win knew who the man was as soon as he said Lady Sarah. He was an Oxford don who lectured on the Ottoman Empire and was always in the social pages because of events he attended with his wife, the daughter of a duke. Thankful that he recalled the man's profession, he said, "Are you heading to Istanbul for research?"

Marchman laughed. "Lord, I can't stand that new name. I much prefer Constantinople, don't you?"

"I can't say I've given it much thought, sir." Win leaned back and puffed on his pipe. "What takes you to the great city?"

"I'm giving a lecture at the Institute. You should come along. Dare I say that I think it would be enlightening?"

"I imagine it would and I may take you up on that offer." Win mulled over the chances of this distinguished man being the one he sought. An Oxford scholar and tutor would be a good cover for a spy. The don would be able to move in and out of various countries at his leisure. He'd only have to set up a lecture somewhere and he would have access to varied groups of people. Win placed that thought aside to mull over later when he was alone.

A blond-haired man pulled out the chair next to Marchman. "May I join you gentlemen?" Without waiting for a response, he sat and lit a cigarette. "I'm Donald Perry."

The don held his hand out to shake Perry's." "Hugo Marchman and this is Winchester Barrington, IV."

"Barrington, huh?" Perry's voice carried through the train even over the sound of the wheels clacking in the background. "I know that name. Any relation to the Connecticut Barringtons?

Win nodded. "That's my family, yes."

"What luck to find you. I've been trying to get in to see someone from your company for years. I have this invention—"

"I say, my man, this is not the time or the place for such things." Marchman said. "Let's enjoy the port and the company without discussing business."

"A man of business like me always thinks it's the right time for discussions about things that will make money." Perry leaned in on one elbow, put his back to Marchman and addressed Win. "What if I go get my device and show it to you? I think it can be beneficial to us both. I'm thinking it was meant to be that we're on the same train."

Win stood. "Please excuse me. I need to go check on

something." He turned to Marchman. "It was nice to meet you. I'm sure we'll see each other again on the journey. Let me know when your lecture is. I'll try to make it." He bowed, turned on his heel, and made his way to the door.

Behind him, Perry called out, "No need to be rude, young man."

Win kept walking, opened the door, and entered the corridor. Under his breath, he muttered, "Great. Trapped on seventy tons of steel with an obnoxious American who doesn't seem to have any manners at all."

"Excuse me sir, did you need something?" a passing steward asked.

Win did a double take, recognized the young man, and said, "No thank you, Lucien. I'm talking to myself. A bad habit, I'm afraid."

"I understand sir. If you need me, just ring. I'm on duty for a little longer and then Remy will be on."

"Thank you." Arriving at his door, Win inserted his key and entered. He flopped down on the made up bed, loosened his tie and kicked off his shoes. What a long trip it was going to be if he had to avoid the obnoxious American. He glanced around the room. Cordelia must have spoken to Lucien about making the beds separately since they weren't pushed together.

∽∾∽

Fiona wasn't ready for bed. She wasn't sure she

wanted to get back out there, with the people she was beginning to think of as sharks, swimming in the water
around a bloody carcass, with her being the victim. She
was in over her head for sure with the rich people on the
train. Why she thought she would be able to fit in was a
mystery. She'd been deluding herself about that, for sure.

Frustrated with herself, she slapped her hand on the
bed and lectured herself. "Get yourself up and get back
out there. You can do this. You're as good as they are.
They're people just like you."

She slipped her shoes back on, left her compartment,
and headed toward the lounge. She knew they were playing card games and, even if no one wanted to talk to her,
she could sit and watch. She had as much right to be there
as they did.

In the lounge, she found several of the ladies sitting
at one of the tables with drinks in front of them. Strange-
ly, there weren't many men around.

"Come over with us, Fiona," Cordelia called out.
"There's plenty of room."

Bracing herself for Cordelia's incessant chatter, Fiona made her way over to the corner where the women sat.

She didn't recognize any of them from her earlier
encounters but they all looked like they were enjoying
themselves. She sat and, when the waiter came, she ordered a gin and tonic.

Cordelia laughed. "Always with the gin, Fi. Why
don't you try something else?"

"Next time then, you order for me."

"I will. You'll love what I order, I promise." Cordelia turned to the woman beside her. "Let me introduce you to these ladies."

Fiona smiled at the older woman seated next to her friend.

Before Cordelia could open her mouth to introduce them, the door to the lounge opened and Lucien came in followed by a group of men and women who were all talking at once and very loudly.

Fiona glanced over toward the noise, just as the bartender called out to Lucien in French. Fiona understood him to say that Lucien wasn't allowed in there.

Lucien didn't respond to the bartender. He staggered across the floor, bumping into tables and chairs on his way across the room.

Fiona, realizing something was wrong with the man, leapt from her own seat. It clattered to the floor. She lunged toward the cabin steward as he fell into the aisle. She caught him right before he landed on his face.

A huge knife stuck out of his back. He opened his mouth to say something and blood gushed out all over Fiona's dress.

Horrified, she looked up at the gathering crowd. It seemed that everyone on the train had followed Lucien into the lounge car.

"Someone get a doctor," she yelled, "He's been stabbed."

"It was the black one," Lucien whispered. "The black one."

His teeth were covered in blood and all Fiona wanted to do was look away but she couldn't. She was pretty sure he was dying and that she was hearing his last words. "What do you mean? Who do you mean?"

He turned his head and coughed up some more blood. This time the liquid coming out was an ebony black and mixed with mucus. "Black. Black." With one last big effort, he grabbed Fiona's skirt, leaving a handprint. "Get the black one."

Puzzled at his words, she glanced around the room to see if anyone else heard his strange sentence. No one appeared to be listening. They all stood in shock at what was happening in front of them.

A large man dressed in an official uniform appeared in front of Fiona. "I have this. I'll take it from here. Let me see what I can do for him."

Fiona stood and moved aside. "I think it's too late. I'm afraid he's gone." Tears filled her eyes, blinding her momentarily. The poor young man. She grieved for him since he'd been so kind to her. She knew his sisters would miss his gentle soul. It was so unfair for his life to be taken from him so soon and in such an awful way.

A group of rail employees took control of the scene and removed Lucien's body.

The passengers remaining in the lounge took seats and began to talk about the tragedy.

Sarah Marchman came over to Fiona. "Hugh and I came in right in time to see you try to assist the young man. I'm sorry you had to have him fall on you like that. He's quite ruined your frock."

"I don't care about the dress. I feel so sorry for the young man. What could he have done to deserve this?"

"One never knows, dear. Did he say anything to you? Did he tell you who did it?"

"No. He said nothing." No way was Fiona going to tell this woman what Lucien said. She'd already decided that she wouldn't talk to anyone but the police. There were a limited number of people on the train and any one of them could have done it.

Fiona only knew for sure that Cordelia, the other ladies at her table, and the two men already in the room when Lucien arrived were innocent.

Anyone else could be the one who did this horrible thing to the poor steward.

Fiona moved over to the bar and ordered a straight glass of gin. Once the bartender poured it, she gulped it down with one swig. She slammed the glass back on the bar and he poured her another. She downed it as well.

"Don't you think that's enough?" Lady Sarah asked.

"No. I don't. I won't be able to sleep after what happened and I want to drink until I forget and pass out."

"That's not a good plan, Fi." Cordelia had come over to the bar. "Let's go talk to Barry about this. You need to get that dress off and to the steward as well, so they can try to get the blood out. Look at it. It's already hard and stiff."

Fiona gaped at Cordelia. "Why are you all so damned worried about my dress? This man is dead. Do you hear me? Did you see it? The man is—dead. Do you think I give one bit of a damn about my gown?" She knew she was bordering on being hysterical but, cripes, did they not care a whit about the dead man?

Cordelia backed away with her hands held up in surrender. "All right. I'll leave you alone to deal with your feelings about this. I'm going to my compartment. If you want me, I'll be there."

"Thanks but don't wait up for me. I plan to get very drunk and fall down in a coma on my bed." Fiona shook her head at Cordelia and turned to the bartender. "Can I get a bottle delivered to my cabin?"

"You can. I'll have Remy bring it around."

"Who's Remy?"

"The night steward."

The mention of the word steward made Fiona burst into tears.

Lady Sarah took her by the arm. "Come on. I'll escort you back to your compartment."

Fiona went willingly and left the noisy, gossipy lounge car behind. The rich folks didn't seem to care about the poor steward but she bet if he was one of their own, they'd be all over someone to figure out who killed him.

For the moment, she was grateful that she was the outsider who actually cared more about people than frocks.

# Chapter 5

When there is no peril in the fight, there is no glory in the triumph. ~ *Pierre Corneille, French Dramatist, 1606-1684*

C ordelia lifted her skirts in an unladylike manner as soon as she left the lounge and dashed down the corridor to her compartment.

She hoped her brother was there since she hadn't seen him since dinner. She turned the key and entered the room. She shut the door behind her and tried to catch her breath.

Win glanced up from his notebook as the door opened. "What's wrong? Your face is ashen." He stood, took a step around the bunk, and then moved toward her.

"That cabin steward Lucien was stabbed. He's dead."
Cordelia's entire body shook as she bent over to ease the
stitch in her side from her flight down the hallway.

Win skidded to a halt. "What? Where?"

"In the lounge." Cordelia sat on the edge of Win's
bed. "It was terrible. Awful."

"Did you see it happen? Who did it?"

"I don't know. He came in while we were having
drinks. He staggered in and the bartender yelled at him
for being where he wasn't supposed to be. Before we
knew it, the steward was falling and blood was all over
the floor and Fiona's dress."

"Fiona's dress?"

"Yeah. Fi was the only one who got up to try to help
the man and he ended up dying all over her. It was hor-
rendous. Blood came out of his mouth and covered her
and the floor. Do you think his murder could have anything to do with your mission?"

"I don't know but I need to head out there and see
what I can find out. Will you be scared here alone?"

"I might be shaken but I'll be all right. We have the
gun, don't we?"

"It's tucked under my clean skivvies on the closet
shelf. Put it where you can reach it and have it in case
you need it." He leaned down and picked up his shoes.
"Try not to use it on me when I get back."

"I'll give it a whirl, dear brother. I'm going to leave
the light on so I'll be sure not to."

"All right. I'm going now." He'd put on and tied his leather shoes and put his dinner jacket back on. "See if you can get some rest."

"I won't sleep until you get back. I can't decide if you need to take the gun with you to protect you or if I need it here."

"I can take care of myself, Cordelia. I'll be back before you know it." He opened the door and went out.

Cordelia paced the room as best she could with the beds made up and wondered idly if Barry told the steward to separate them and if he told that crazy pregnancy story as the reason why. As soon as she had the thought, the enormity of what had happened and the fact that the man who made her bed earlier had died such a violent death right in front of her hit her. She doubled over and sobbed.

She couldn't decide if she were crying for the man himself or for the trauma of what she'd witnessed. She knew she was self-centered but she sincerely hoped that she was crying for the man.

కుడి

Win made his way down the corridor toward the lounge. Concerned that the steward had been killed because he'd seen or heard something he shouldn't have. Win was curious to see if he could find out who had been in the lounge when the murder happened, as opposed to who had been unaccounted for at that time.

Sad as it might be that the man was dead, the list of who Win himself should be looking to find might be shortened by this incident.

If the man's death was related to Win's mission, anyone who was in the bar area at the time could be scratched off his list of suspects. There would be no way for them to be the culprit.

Arriving at the lounge, Win pushed the door open with the palm of his hand and entered. The place was abuzz with chatter about the stabbing of the steward.

Noticing Hugo Marchman seated near the man who had leapt on the train as it left the station, Win worked his way through the tables and joined them. "What ho, Marchman? Any news on who's responsible for the death of Lucien?"

Before Marchman could answer, the other man held his hand out. "Mack Plant. Remember me?"

"I sure do. How are you?"

Plant glanced around the room. "There's lots of work to do here to find out what exactly is going on. I see a number of possibilities but the good news is that there's not a lot of people who could have done it, since the train has been moving for a while and the only person or persons who could have done the deed have been onboard since Paris.

"No one has gotten off either so the pool of suspects is finite. I only hope that the railway company doesn't let anyone debark at the next station."

"You sound like you've been mulling this over for a bit. I hope you're right about the company not letting anyone off." Win wondered why this Plant man was so in touch with the ways of investigating crimes. Was he a policeman?

"I would think that they won't. They sure don't want the rail company to have bad publicity. I predict they will have law enforcement get on at the next stop and question everyone on board."

Hugo raised his hand to get a waiter's attention and made a circular motion for refills for him and Plant.

He turned to Win. "What're you drinking, Barrington?"

"Whiskey. I've gotten quite used to it, I'm afraid."

"What does that mean?" Plant asked.

"Ahh, see, I came of age when Prohibition was in and we drank a lot of whiskey in an iced tea glass to pass it off as legal." Win laughed. "Dad had it served at dinner each night."

"Better watch out," Hugo pointed his cigarette in Plant's direction. "This guy's a cop from Chicago. He could run you in."

"I highly doubt that. The statute of limitations has run and we all know that Chicago was the center of Prohibition excesses. I probably didn't do anything that the good citizens of that city haven't." Win looked over at Plant. "If you're from Chicago, why the British accent?"

"Ever heard of undercover work?" Plant asked.

"You're not much of a pro at it if you've already told Marchman and me that you're American and law enforcement to boot."

"I could be feeding you both a load of hokey. For all you know, I'm from Cambridgeshire and have lived there my whole life running a punting company."

Hugo traded his used glass for the full one the waiter held out. "No, Mr. Plant. That's not possible at all. Remember, I'm from Oxford and I think I can spot a Cambridge man from fifty paces. You're American, all right."

Win pulled out his notebook and pencil. "Do you think it would do any good to try talking to people to see who was actually in the room when Lucien was killed? At least we could have those people that couldn't have done it narrowed down when the authorities arrive."

Using the palm of his hand to wipe the condensation from his glass, Plant said, "Are you a cop yourself then, Barrington?"

Embarrassed at his gaffe, Win said, "Oh, no, no. Just an amateur sleuth. You know, I like to read those whodunits even if some of them are pretty dreadful. I thought it might be interesting to take a stab—forgive the pun—at seeing if I could narrow the field of suspects."

"Good luck with that, chap. If you'll forgive me, I'm going out to get some fresh air. I find I like to stand at the juncture of two cars and take in the breeze." Mack Plant stood and downing his drink in one gulp, slammed the glass down onto the white tablecloth. "Good evening, gentlemen." He turned and walked away.

Win glanced up at Hugo. "Was it something I said?"

"I don't know, old chap. The gentleman seems a bit touchy, doesn't he?"

"He sure does, but enough about him. Any idea who was in here when Lucien was killed?"

"From what I've heard, it was mostly the ladies. Maybe a few men but most of us were still out having our port."

"Or out stabbing someone in the corridor." Win snapped his notebook shut. "I think I'll head outside myself."

Hugo stood. "I'll accompany you if you don't mind. I think it's pretty stuffy in here and I could use a walk."

"I don't mind at all."

Win really did mind. He wanted to use the time to meander around the train a little and see what he could find out, but he'd been raised to be polite and didn't want to offend the don.

Before they arrived at the door to the corridor, the Frenchman, Jacques Cassel stopped them in their tracks. "Good evening, *monsieurs*. Interesting night, no?"

"It is indeed, *Monsieur* Cassel. I guess you heard about the steward." Hugo inclined his head toward Win. "Barrington and I are on our way out to get some fresh air. Perhaps you'd like to join us?"

"That would be superb. I would like that very much.

I'd be interested to hear your theories on the killing, Professor."

"I'm not sure why since my expertise is actually on the Ottoman Empire not murder but I'll be glad to chat about the events of the evening."

Win led the way out of the lounge car. Curious to hear what the Frenchman had to say, he held the door open for the other two men and once they were in the corridor, he followed along behind them. Cassel unwrapped a peppermint on their way to the end of the car and stashed the paper in his suit coat pocket.

# Chapter 6

*The truth is rarely pure, and never simple. ~ Oscar Wilde, Irish Dramatist, 1854-1900*

Fiona pulled on her silk nightgown and combed her hair before plaiting it for the night. She always slept with her hair that way, since she tossed and turned a lot and woke with snarls in her tresses if she didn't tie them back. More than once she'd contemplated getting a short cut but was afraid it would make her look even more like her mother and she certainly didn't want that.

She placed her peignoir at the foot of the bed. She almost didn't pack it since she wasn't sharing her compartment but she decided she might need it if there was a fire, a train derailment or something unexpected. She also hadn't realized that there were conductors sitting at the end of each carriage and that they would see her if she needed to use the facilities in the night.

She patted it, grateful that she'd thrown it in her suitcase.

The pillowcase and sheets were divine. She slid her body inside the covers and let out a deep sigh. Lovely. So lovely.

Before she could get more comfortable, a knock at her door startled her into a seated position. What now?

Deciding to ignore it, she turned onto her side and closed her eyes.

The knocking got louder.

Fiona flung the covers off, and sat up. "I'm asleep," she called out. "Please call back in the morning. I don't want to be disturbed."

The knocking continued.

Frustrated, Fiona grabbed her peignoir and tossed it across her shoulders. She unlocked the hinge and jerked the door open. "What?"

"Let me in, Fi. It's freezing out here."

"What are you doing, Cordelia? Why aren't you in bed? It's late."

Cordelia barged past Fiona and into the compartment. "How can you even think about sleeping? There's been a murder on the train. Don't you want to figure out who did it?"

"No, quite frankly, I don't." Fiona closed the door. "I liked Lucien but I'm not an expert on murders and I think it's best to leave that kind of thing to the police. Right now, I want to go to sleep."

Cordelia laughed. "That reminds me. When I first knocked, you yelled, 'I'm asleep.' That's crazy. You can't be asleep and say that."

"Please go back to your own compartment. I'll see you tomorrow and we can talk then. I'm really tired."

"Get dressed. Come on. It'll be an adventure."

"I'm afraid that's not a good idea. In case you don't remember, this person you're seeking is dangerous and the best thing we can do is leave it to the authorities. It's not an adventure. It's practically suicide."

"Pshaw. I have this under control. Our killer used a knife. I have this." Cordelia whipped a small pistol out of her jacket pocket and waved it around. "Hurry up. Get dressed. Let's go."

"You're insane. Give me that gun. You're going to kill yourself or me if you don't stop flinging it about."

"I guess I was mistaken. I thought that since you were brave enough to board this train in the first place, as a single woman headed all the way to Istanbul that you were up for adventures. You really disappoint me, Fiona." Cordelia turned on her heel and reached out to open the compartment door.

"Wait just a minute. Let me put on my robe and I'll walk you down to the conductor so he can make sure you get back to your cabin. I'm surprised your husband was agreeable to you traipsing through the corridors like a madwoman."

"You don't have to insult me. Barry has no idea that I'm even out of the compartment."

"I don't mean to insult you but if you think about it for a few minutes, it's pretty reckless behavior. Tell you what, tomorrow, we'll put our heads together and try to figure out who could've done it. I really think we'd do better on a full night's sleep." Fiona tried to take Cordelia's arm but the other woman pulled away from her and flounced out the door.

Fiona followed her and poked her head out into the hallway. She called out, "You're going the wrong way."

"I never said I was going back to my compartment. You said that. I don't have to do what you say. Watch me. I'm going to investigate." Cordelia walked out of sight as she said the words.

Fiona hesitated for a few moments undecided on what to do. Concern for her new friend made her want to follow but her own fear paralyzed her a bit. She wasn't sure about how to find Barry since Cordelia said he wasn't in their compartment.

Frustrated but concerned, Fiona finally decided she'd have better luck following Cordelia and trying to stop her crazy errand than to try to find the woman's husband. She sighed, walked out of the cabin, and closed the door.

She passed by the conductor seated at the end of the

corridor and smiled at him as she opened the door to the next carriage. Upon stepping into that area, she noticed the door at the far end shutting.

Finding it hard to believe that Cordelia could move that fast, but not seeing her, Fiona increased her own pace to try to catch up with her friend. Her gown fluttered behind her as she practically ran through the next sleeper car. She got almost to the end of the corridor when a compartment door opened startling her.

She turned to find Johnny Rozzelle standing there. "Ahh, it's one of my lovely dinner companions." He quirked his brow. "And in her nightie, too. How unlucky for me that I have to get to a meeting, otherwise I'd invite you in and we could have a real nice time."

Appalled, Fiona stepped back. "How dare you say such a thing to me?"

"I have to tell you though, my dear, I'd take great joy in taking your hair down from that plait if I had a chance. Maybe tomorrow night?"

"You're crazy. I'm not out here looking for a man. My friend Cordelia ran past here and I was trying to catch up to her. Go on to your meeting and leave me alone." Fiona took a step toward the door beside where the conductor sat, studiously ignoring the two first class passengers. They'd been trained to serve but to do so unobtrusively.

Rozzelle grabbed Fiona's upper arm and peered into her face. "Little lady, you're on the wrong side of your compartment door dressed provocatively. I suggest you get yourself back behind the door lock on your cabin before someone molests you."

"I have to get Cordelia and believe me, once I do, I plan on doing just that. Now, let me pass."

"Listen to me. You're not paying attention. You had better not go any farther or you could be in danger. This is the end of the first class area and you have no idea what's on the other side of that door there." He pointed at the exit.

"But my friend—"

"Forget your friend if you want to be safe. I'm telling you, little lady, it's dangerous out there and I can guarantee that your friend has already probably found that danger."

"Then I truly must go and get her."

"You seem not to want to see the sun rise, missy. I'm telling you, only the worst of people are up and about at this time of night brokering deals of the kind that have been done on this train since it started running over a half a century ago. Go back to your safe little room and go to bed."

"How dare you tell me what to do, you insufferable—"

Instead of letting her finish her sentence, Rozzelle jerked Fiona to his chest and grabbed a wad of the fabric of her gown and robe in his fist. He pressed his lips on hers and tried to poke his tongue in her mouth.

She kicked his shin and twisted away from him so fast that she heard the fabric of her nightgown tear.

Unaware of how big the rip might be, since she couldn't see it for the tears welling in her eyes, she ran blindly down the corridor back in the direction of her own compartment.

Once she arrived at her door, she unlocked it and entered the room. She quickly found a sheet of paper and wrote a note to Cordelia's husband telling him what had happened. Haunted by the fact that she let that man Rozzelle dissuade her from her mission, she had to admit, after taking a minute to catch her breath, that he may have been right and that parading down the corridors in her nightgown wasn't really a good idea.

Fiona gave the note to the sleeper car attendant in the hallway. She gave him a small tip to deliver it and went back to her compartment. She paced for a while, hoping to hear back from Mr. Barrington but, after half an hour, she fell back on her bed and, after tossing a bit, finally fell into a light sleep.

ℯↄℯↄ

When Win arrived at his compartment a little after three a.m., he was stunned to see Cordelia's bunk empty and undisturbed. She hadn't even lain down. *Damn her hide. She's probably out cavorting with someone and making me look like a man who can't control his wife.*

He knew he shouldn't have trusted her to behave. Who knew how long she'd been gone since he'd gotten stuck for way too long watching the American Donald Perry try to out drink and out gamble the Frenchman, Jacques Cassel.

Win stayed and watched in case one of the men said something to assist him in his investigation but it was a colossal waste of time. The only thing the late night game did for him was make him curious how the Cassel man could eat so many peppermints while he drank prodigious amounts of scotch. By the time the game was over, the table was littered with empty glasses, full ashtrays, and a pile of candy wrappers. Tired and grouchy, all Win wanted to do was sleep.

He tugged off his tie and undid his cufflinks. Tossing them on the side table, he picked up the note that had been set there and opened it. The writing was too neat to be Cordelia's and he glanced to the end. It was signed Fiona Vancleave. Well, that was a relief. She must be writing to say that Cordelia was staying with her.

He started at the beginning of the letter and his heart sank as he read. He ran his hands through his hair. His sister had always been reckless and now she was probably hurt or worse. That mule-headedness of hers was going to be her undoing.

He had a swift thought of how he would break the news to his mother if something had happened to Cordelia.

He straightened his spine. His sister was his responsibility and he was going to get her back.

Win left his compartment stepping over to the car attendant. He asked him to go find the chief conductor and send him to the end of the first class compartment. That was where the note said that Fiona had last seen Cordelia.

Determined to have the entire train searched for his sister, Win strode that way himself. He hoped to find Cordelia without disturbing Fiona's rest but if he had to wake her, he would.

He and the conductor went through the second-class compartments and didn't find any trace of Cordelia. The conductor enlisted additional assistance in the search and they quickly covered all areas of the train, including the storage areas for the food, wine, and baggage. No signs of Cordelia anywhere.

Terrified of what could have happened to his sister, Win made his way to Fiona's compartment at five fifteen a.m. hoping that Cordelia had somehow returned there while they were searching the back of the train. If Cordelia wasn't with Fiona, Win planned to rejoin the conductor and assist in the search of the other first class compartments. He tapped on Fiona's door. When she didn't answer, he knocked louder. He could hear someone moving around inside and banged on the door with the side of his fist. "Open the door."

"Who is it?"

"It's Winchester Barrington. Is Cordelia in there?"

The door opened and Fiona peered out. "Didn't you get my note?"

"I did and I'm looking for Cordelia."

"It's five in the morning. Are you just now getting concerned about your wife? She told me that she planned to divorce you but this seems cold even for someone who doesn't love his wife. She's been missing for a number of hours now and you're just now showing up?"

"Let me in please. I need to talk to you but I don't want to announce my business out in the corridor."

She stepped back and held the door open for him to pass through. She tugged her robe tighter around herself.

He stepped over the threshold embarrassed a bit by coming into her sleeping chambers. The covers were still mussed from where she had lain, and so he averted his eyes from the bed.

Fiona leaned against the wall of the compartment. "Why are you here, Mr. Barrington?"

"I told you. I'm looking for Cordelia."

"As you can see, she isn't here." Fiona waved her hand around to encompass the room. "I assure you, sir, there's no place in this compartment to hide your wife."

"When did you last see her?"

"Did you even *read* my note?"

"I did but I want to hear the actual details from you."

"Look, your wife, whom you obviously dislike from the way you treat her and the way you've delayed trying to find her, came here to my cabin, looking for someone to come along on her *investigation* of the stabbing of Lucien. I tried to tell her it was a fool's errand and that she needed to leave it to the professionals, but she insisted that she was going with or without me. I gave in and followed her."

"You gave in?"

"Of course, I did. You know very well how she is. She's a wild thing. She can't be dissuaded once she has a plan in place. I imagine that was what first attracted you to her and why you wanted to marry her only to tire of that behavior early in your marriage."

"Will you stop with the marriage thing?" Win flopped down on the bed he'd been trying to ignore and placed his head in his hands. All he really wanted to do was scream over and over again until someone produced his sister.

"Stop what?"

He looked up at her with what he knew to be anguish on his face. It had to be there since he was feeling it so acutely. "Stop saying those awful things about her. I love her. I've loved her all my life and I can't bear to think about something bad having happened to her."

"If you love her so much, why are you just now looking for her? And why are you so mean to her?" Fiona looked like some kind of avenging angel as she stood with her hands on her hips with her hair escaping from her braid and curling around her head as if it were a halo.

"I've been scouring the train, along with a team of conductors, for hours. There's no sign of her and so I came here to see if you had any additional information that could help."

"I'm sorry that I don't. I wish I did." Fiona relaxed her posture a bit then sat beside Win. "I'm glad to hear that you love her. I can see by how upset you are that you truly do care for her. Maybe you can talk her out of the divorce—you could try to woo her back once we find her. She can't have gone far. The train isn't that big."

"I'm scared she's dead." As the words left his lips, he knew they could very well be true. His heart constricted and he thought he might throw up. What if she'd died because she found out something about the person he was trying to uncover as a murderous spy? How could he go on living if he got his sister killed?

Fiona gasped. "I hope not. I think she'll turn up safe and sound. We have to hope so. Don't give up."

Ignoring her optimism, his eyes searched her face. "What will I tell my mother?"

"*Your* mother? What do you mean? Wouldn't you be worried about telling *her* parents if something happened to her?"

"Her parents are *my* parents."

"Huh?" Fiona tilted her head in confusion then she nodded. "You think of her parents as your own. That's so sweet."

"No." Win grabbed Fiona's hands. "They *are* my parents. Cordelia is my sister. She's not my wife."

"What are you talking about? I think you're so distraught you can't think straight. I have some sedatives in my purse. Let me get one for you."

Fiona started to rise. Win pulled her back down.

"No. She really is my sister. She came on the train posing as my wife, to help me out and now our charade may have cost her life. Don't you see? How can I live with myself if I've lost her?"

"You've got to stop thinking that way. We have to be positive. She's going to show up."

"I hope you're right."

A banging at the door startled Win. He jumped as if a shot went off.

Fiona rose and walked over to the door and opened it.

The chief conductor stood in the opening. "We've found your wife or at least we think it's her."

Win's blood ran cold. "Think?"

"There's no way to be sure yet but I think we'll know quite soon. I'm waiting on word now."

"Dear God, man, why don't we know? What's the hold up?"

Fiona touched Win's arm. "Calm down, let's see what the conductor has to say. Ranting at the man isn't going to help."

"Just tell me, sir, is my sister alive or dead?"

# Chapter 7

I know that's a secret, for it's whispered everywhere. ~ *William Congreve, English Dramatist,*
*1670-1729*

An unconscious but alive woman was found on
the embankment almost seventy miles back,"
the chief conductor said. "The farmer who
found her took her to the closest medical facility and
when the doctors saw her clothing, they surmised she
might have fallen off the train since she was dressed in an
expensive gown. They called the stationmaster at the local tracks and when they heard from our telegrams that
we had lost a passenger, they radioed this information to
us."

"What are you doing about it?" Win asked.

"I've got someone headed over to the hospital to see if the woman is awake now and if it's indeed your wife."

"And if it is?" Fiona asked.

"We'll either arrange for her to be brought to the next stop if she's able or we'll let Mr. Barrington here make arrangements for his wife's—wait, did you call her your *sister*?"

"Mr. Barrington's distraught. He misspoke. He meant his wife."

Fiona didn't know why she was lying for Win but she somehow knew it was important to keep his cover story intact. She wasn't normally one for lies and subterfuge but for some reason this man and his sister had become important to her.

The conductor shook his head. "I don't know how he'd get a wife and a sister confused but whatever you say, ma'am." He reached for the doorknob. "Once I hear back from the stationmaster, I'll come let you know if it's Mrs. Barrington." The man stressed the word Mrs. as if he were still a bit unsure of the lady's status.

Win reached out and shook the man's hand. "Please do let me know as soon as you hear. I'm eager to find out and I'm hopeful that this woman is my wife and that she will regain consciousness soon."

"Will you be here then, sir?"

"Oh, no. I should say not. Miss Vancleave must get dressed but I hope she will join me for breakfast in the restaurant car and we will be there together." Win turned to Fiona. "Will you break your fast with me when you're ready?"

She nodded. "I'll be right there. I want to know about Cordelia as soon as possible."

The two men left Fiona alone in the compartment. She pulled off her nightgown, inspected the hole that Rozzelle's attentions had torn in it and sighed. Something else to mend. This trip was turning out to be a rough one as far as her wardrobe went.

She dressed for the day in a brown suede skirt and a white button-front blouse. She tossed on a jacket that matched the skirt then slid on her hosiery and shoes before making her way down the corridor. As she walked, she wondered what the deal was with the Barringtons. Why would they pretend to be married? It seemed a little—no, a lot—odd.

Determined to find out some answers, Fiona strode down the hallway at a fast clip. She almost ran into Lady Sarah Marchman when the train took an unexpected curve. Grabbing the wall to steady herself, Fiona apologized. "I'm so sorry. I guess by the time I get used to this thing moving, we'll be in Istanbul."

"It's quite all right, dear. I'm the same way. It takes a bit of work to get your legs under you. Almost like being at sea, I think, don't you?"

"You're probably right. Someone else said that to me last night. It must be true."

"I'm on my way to breakfast. Would you care to join me?"

"I wish I could but I promised Winchester Barrington that I'd eat with him this morning." Fiona smiled at the older lady, who she really liked and would love to emulate. Lady Sarah was so poised and dignified and Fiona envied her that.

"Really? Barrington? Hmm. What about that beautiful wife of his? Is she turning him over to you? I hardly see Cordelia Barrington as the husband-sharing type."

Fiona almost choked. She'd never even thought about what people on the train would think when they saw her eating alone with a married man. Oh Lord, now what was she going to do?

Lady Sarah laughed and placed a hand on Fiona's arm. "It's all right, dear. No one will think anything bad of you."

Fiona's skin seemed to burn from the inside out. "How'd you know that was what I was thinking?"

"I could tell by the horrified look on your face. No need to fret. Everyone will know it's innocent. I daresay they couldn't think otherwise." Lady Sarah moved forward, keeping her hand in place. "Come on. We'll go in together."

Fiona accompanied Lady Sarah, slightly upset that the woman thought there would be no way that Winchester Barrington, who Fiona couldn't help but think of as Win, would be interested in her. True, Cordelia was beautiful in a way that Fiona could never hope to be but still, it was hurtful for Mrs. Marchman to make that clear to her. In the nicest way possible, of course.

The aristocracy had always had a way of making the common class feel inferior and put in their place, while exercising the best possible manners.

Upon entering the restaurant car, Fiona glanced around to see where Win was seated. He'd chosen a table for two near the end of the car and in front of a window. "Great," she mumbled under her breath, "looks like a tete-a-tete. Wonderful."

She approached the table where Win sat with his coffee already in front of him. When she was beside the other chair, he leapt up to pull hers out for her. "Allow me."

"Do you think this is a good idea?" Fiona asked, without sitting down.

"What?"

"You've chosen a place that's secluded and I'm a single girl seated with a married man. People may talk."

He burst into laughter. "No, they won't. Come, sit. It's fine."

The stress of worrying about Cordelia, combined with the run-in with Rozzelle the evening before and her feelings of inadequacy after Lady Sarah's comments, caught up to her and Fiona burst into tears. Embarrassed at her lack of control, she spun on her heel and tried to escape to the corridor.

Before she got three steps, Win waylaid her with a

hand on her elbow. "What's wrong? Why are you so upset?"

Tears flowing down her face, she glared up at him. "I know I'm not the prettiest girl and I'm not elegant but I'm at least worthy of respect even if you don't think I am."

He held his hands up in a gesture of surrender. "Whoa. Where did that come from?"

"Never mind. I'm leaving. Send me a note when you find out what's going on with Cordelia."

"Please sit down. I wanted to thank you for what you did for me today, when you told that conductor that I was distraught and made a mistake. It's vital that no one know that Cordelia and I aren't married. It could be a matter of life and death."

Intrigued, Fiona went back to the chair and sat. "Tell me what you mean." She wiped her face with the heels of her hands and, taking the napkin at her place-setting, opened it and blotted her eyes.

"This really isn't the place. We need to be alone."

"Well, well, little lady. You wouldn't return my kiss last night but you're willing to sit here with this married man brashly in the light of day discussing being alone with him," Johnny Rozzelle said as he came to a stop beside their table.

Win half-rose. "What the hell are you talking about, Rozzelle? How dare you insult this lady."

"*Me* insult her? *Me?*" Rozzelle pointed at Win.

"You're a married man with your wife right down the corridor and you're setting up an assignation right under her nose. Shame on *you*, sir."

Fiona was ready to slap both men for the way they were acting. "Nobody's setting up anything. All I wanted to do was have some eggs and ham in peace. Now, may I have it here or do I have to move to another table?"

In response, Win snapped his fingers and called the waiter over. "The lady would like eggs and ham." He turned to Fiona. "How do you like them cooked?"

"Sunnyside up, please."

"Anything else?" the waiter asked.

"Yes, please, we'd like some coffee and a selection of pastries." Fiona turned to Rozzelle. "Please excuse us. We have some things to discuss."

"This isn't over, little lady. I'm not so easily discouraged especially since I now see exactly what kind of girl you really are."

"You're despicable. Get away from me." Fiona practically spat out the words. She knew she'd never sleep again on the train for worrying about this man coming uninvited to her compartment; but she wasn't going to sit quietly and take his nastiness.

"Mr. Rozzelle, you and I are going to have a serious discussion when the lady isn't present. You're going to apologize to her for the way you've spoken to her and for the way you've behaved, if you have acted improperly."

"Bring it on right now, Barrington, if you think

you're able to. You have no idea who you're messing around with, mister," Rozzelle snarled.

"Look. It's early in the day after a late night. Let's agree to settle this after we each have a chance to have breakfast and digest the meal. Then all bets will be off." Win smiled a smile that scared Fiona breathless. The man who seemed so dignified appeared to have an animal side to him.

At the look on Win's face, Rozzelle backed away. "I'll see you later then, Barrington. It's a promise."

As soon as he was gone, Fiona said, "Are you sure you want to tangle with him? I think he's involved in illegal things."

"I'm quite sure he is but that's neither here nor there. What did he mean about returning his kiss?"

"When I was chasing after Cordelia last night, he cut me off and grabbed me. He said I was inviting men to do that by being out in the corridor in my nightgown. Cordelia didn't give me a chance to change and I was trying to get her to come to her senses. I'm afraid I darted out of my compartment without even thinking about what I was wearing." A sob escaped her lips. "He tore my gown."

Win slammed his palm down on the table. "Did he hurt you?"

"No." Fiona shook her head. "Nothing like that. I'm scared of him, though. He's creepy and I'm sure he's a criminal."

"We'll see what we can do about having someone

watch your compartment since you're alone. I wouldn't want anything to happen to you. You've been such a good friend to Cordelia." He paused, reached over and squeezed her hand that was on the table. "And me."

The waiter chose that time to appear with their food. Win let go of Fiona's hand. She was sure someone would pass the word on the train that she'd been holding hands with a married man, but for that brief second, she didn't care. His hand was warm and comforting and exactly what she needed in that moment. She pushed any thought of it meaning anything other than gratitude to the back of her mind.

"Eat up." Win nodded at her plate. "Let's hope we get some news soon about Cordelia."

"I also want to have that conversation we need to be alone to have."

"I promise that we will. I have a feeling it's going to be a long day so we need to be sure to be ready to face what's ahead." Win scooped some of his eggs onto his fork and took a large bite.

As she ate, Fiona watched him and thought about what it would be like for him to court her. Her opinion of him had changed from when he was being so rude to Cordelia earlier on the trip. He really was a nice man and seemed very concerned about the proper treatment of women.

She suppressed a giggle at that thought, since she'd been the very one to think, just the day before, that he was awful and treated women terribly. What a difference a few hours could make.

As they finished their pastries, the chief conductor came across the room to their table. "We have good news. Cordelia Barrington is the woman they found. She does have a broken arm and some scrapes and abrasions but she's going to be fine. She's awake and has confirmed that she was a passenger on the train. She's giving a statement about what happened to the police and they will have her driven to Vienna to catch up with the train there."

Fiona smiled at the conductor. "Thank God she's all right."

"So we'll see her in a couple of hours when we reach Vienna?" Win asked.

"Barring any delays in her statement or getting her to the station, yes. She also had a message she wanted related to you, sir."

"What did she say?"

"She said not to worry about her but that there were some things she needed you to know as soon as possible. She asked that you be waiting at the closest entrance to your compartment when we pull into the station. She was adamant that you meet her near the platform."

"Did she say anything else? Like why?" Win asked.

"No, but to tell you the truth, sir, she sounded a bit scared, if you know what I mean."

"Of course she was scared. She somehow fell off the

train," Fiona said. Both men turned to stare at her. She put her hand to her mouth as the truth dawned. "Ooh, you think she was pushed?"

Win shook his head. "Shh. Don't say that too loudly. We don't know who may be listening."

"Oh God." Fiona reached for her now tepid coffee and gulped some down. What had she gotten herself into? A man who was most certainly a criminal had tried to seduce or rape her in the corridor. The person she'd befriended had most likely been shoved off the train by yet another criminal. What kind of luxury train was this anyway? It was more like a den of sin.

"Come on, Fiona. Let's get out of here and to a place where we can talk." Win placed his napkin on the table and shoved his chair back. "Thank you, conductor, and we'll be near the platform to greet Mrs. Barrington. I appreciate the work you and your men have done." He reached into his pocket and handed the man a wad of bills.

"Thank you sir and the Wagons-Lit Company apologizes for any inconvenience. We will, of course, pay for the medical treatment and transport of your wife."

"Thank you." Win held his hand out for Fiona. She took his and rose from her seat. There was that warmth again.

Win let go of her hand and she preceded him across the restaurant. Before they exited, her eyes glanced across the room as she sensed someone staring a hole through her back. She couldn't help but look. It was Johnny Roz-zelle with a smirk on his face.

⌘

Win led Fiona to his compartment even though he knew he shouldn't. It wasn't proper for her to be there alone with him, but he needed to talk to her to secure her cooperation without anyone being able to overhear them. He was relieved that Cordelia would soon be back onboard and he could then re-establish his cover story. Fiona was right. It was a bit awkward for him to have invited the single woman to breakfast and then to pick that out of the way table.

He blamed himself for the mistakes. He had to take ownership of them since it was his mission, but he also knew he'd been truly distraught over his missing sister. He knew his bosses at the War Department would never understand and he was hopeful that they would never find out. It was urgent that they didn't. There was no telling what would happen if he failed in his task. War loomed on the horizon and this particular threat needed to be neutralized.

Fiona stopped before entering the compartment. "Do you think this is wise? People will talk."

"I don't think there's anyone around."

"Then get in there fast and I'll follow. We'll have to shut the blinds so no one can see in."

Win went in and she followed. She sat on the couch on one side of the cabin while Win closed the blinds.

He sat opposite her. "Do you think the blinds shut is better than open? If someone looked in, they could see we were both fully dressed and no hanky-panky is going on."

"But they would also see a single girl and a married man who's wife isn't here—and believe me, they are all going to find out she fell off when she shows up with a cast on her arm. They may even think we ganged up and pushed her off so we could be free to be together. That would be awful but I bet that's what the other passengers will say."

"You've read too many crime novels, Miss Librarian."

"Oh, I think not." Fiona laughed. "You and I both know that people love to gossip. The story of the cheating husband and his mistress killing the wife is as old as time immemorial. Think back to the days of the first Queen Elizabeth. Remember the murder of the Earl of Essex's wife?"

"Point taken. The blinds stay closed."

"Tell me why you and Cordelia are pretending to be married in the first place. It seems a little odd."

"She's assisting me in a mission."

"What kind of mission?" Fiona giggled a little. "Surely you're not a spy, are you?"

"Uh."

Fiona leaned against the back of the seat. "No way. You can't be. You're a wealthy businessman, aren't you?"

"I come from a family of entrepreneurs, yes, but I also work for the War Department."

"The United States War Department?"

Win nodded. "Yes. The very one."

"But we're not at war."

"Not yet, but it's coming. Within the next few years, mark my words. There's too much dissension in Europe and there will definitely be war. We want to be ready."

"I can't believe it. I don't want to believe it." Fiona shook her head.

"Whether you want to believe or not, it's coming. Sooner rather than later. This trip I'm on is to learn the lay of the land and find out some information about certain individuals. I'm sorry I can't tell you more. I'm risking a lot by telling you what I am but I wanted you to understand why Cordelia is pretending to be my wife."

"Why is it? You still haven't said."

"I needed the cover of being a newlywed and since I didn't want to be in a compartment with a stranger from the War Department, I asked if I could bring my sister along and to my shock, they agreed. I think part of it was that she already had papers with a name to match mine and they didn't have to try to find a trained agent who could pass as an upper class young woman."

"Is that so hard?"

"What?"

"Passing for upper class?"

"You know what I meant." Great. Now he'd offended her. When would he learn that he couldn't be totally honest with women? They were so sensitive. He needed to fix this before she walked out in a snit.

"No, what *did* you mean?"

"It's just that some of the upper class women are very judgmental of other women and handling their cattiness is a difficult thing to learn in a short time. Women who are born to that lifestyle seem to take to it naturally."

"And women who aren't?"

"Well, I don't want to hurt anyone's feelings, but sadly, I've seen some nice young women reduced to tears over the meanness of some of the women of my class. I wouldn't wish that on anyone."

"I guess I can see your point. I also imagine that it would be hard to share a compartment with someone you didn't know." Fiona glanced around. "Especially since they are quite small, aren't they?"

"It was a good plan at first but now I see how stupid I was. I endangered my sister's life and that was really dumb. First rate idiocy." Win leaned forward and put his head in his hands.

Fiona put her arm across his shoulders. "I'm so sorry that Cordelia got either pushed off the train or fell, but really, she has to carry some of the blame. She wanted to find out who killed Lucien and she wouldn't wait for the officials to do the investigation. She should have been safely ensconced in your compartment while you did your job. If she'd stayed here, she would have been fine."

"Regardless of that, she was on this train because I invited her. I, who know more about her impulsiveness than anyone, thought I could rein her in long enough to get to Istanbul. What a dolt I am."

Fiona reached under his chin and, with her index finger, raised his face to hers. Looking him in the eye, she said, "Stop beating yourself up. You did what you had to do and she's all right. You and I both know that Cordelia herself won't blame you a bit for any of it. She's going to think she went on an adventure. I won't be at all surprised if she got back on this train gleeful and excited about the last several hours."

The train squealed to a stop. "I guess we're about to find out, aren't we? It seems we're in Vienna."

# Chapter 8

Rejoice with your family in the beautiful land of life! *Albert Einstein, German Physicist, 1879-1955*

Several new passengers boarded at Vienna as well as a group of policemen. The passengers who had started in Paris and intended to debark in Vienna, were herded together and taken into the station offices in order to be questioned about the death of the steward as well as the accident involving Cordelia Barrington.

Fiona watched the process of debarkation of the passengers by law enforcement. She stood just inside the door of the train, searching the area for Cordelia. Win got off and walked around on the platform. As he paced, he smoked a pipe. The sweet scent of the tobacco wafted over his head and back into the doorway where Fiona waited.

They waited for a long time with no sign of Cordelia. Win eventually came back to Fiona. "I'm afraid she must have been delayed. I think she's not going to make it in time."

"Then they will have to take her to the next stop, won't they?"

"They will but I'd rather get her back on sooner rather than later. I want her where I can keep an eye on her."

Fiona forced herself not to say that he'd already not been able to keep an eye on his sister. There was no use in pouring salt in his wounds. He'd already beat himself up too much as it was.

"I guess it's almost time to pull out. We may as well return to my compartment."

"I think I'll go back to my own for a while. I think that would be best." She smiled to let him know she wasn't mad but that she had a reputation to protect. Such that it still was.

He nodded. "That's probably for the best. I'll send a note if I hear from Cordelia."

Fiona turned away as the wheels of the train started to move slowly forward. Disappointed that Cordelia didn't make it back and more than a little curious about what exactly had happened to her, Fiona knew it would be a while before the next stop and she really wanted to get the story on Cordelia's adventure. Her shoulders slumped as she moved in the direction of her cabin.

"Hey, ho. Wait a second, Fiona."

"What?" Fiona glanced back at Win. "We're moving. What's going on?"

Win had half his body hanging out the door of the train while he held onto the bar on the outer edge of the car. "Here she comes."

"Do you mean Cordelia?" Fiona stepped over to the stairs. She leaned forward, peering over Win's side, in time to see a man dressed in a station employee's uniform jogging alongside the train, her friend with him.

"Help the lady aboard," the man called out.

He pushed Cordelia up to the entrance and Win took her by the arm that was not in a sling. Fiona reached out to assist as Win's arm snaked around his sister's waist and he swung her onto the step with him.

Once they got her aboard, the man on the platform waved. "Good luck, *fraulein*."

Win scooped Cordelia into his arms and held her to him. "Thank God you're all right."

"Let me go. I'm in pain," she gasped and pulled away from him slightly.

He held her at arm's length and inspected her. "Look at you. Your dress is torn and your stockings are gone." He leaned down and touched her calf. "Scraped. Is this all the damage?"

"Try falling off a train, dear, and see how you turn out. My arm hurts, I'm aware of every rib, and it hurts to breathe. I also have bruises on top of bruises but I'm lucky to be alive. The area where I fell wasn't as bad as it could have been. Thank God we weren't on the top of a mountain at the time."

"You sound awfully upbeat about what happened," Fiona said.

Cordelia peered over Win's shoulder at Fiona. "I am. I'm alive. What could be better?" Cordelia let out an infectious laugh. "What an adventure I've had. Come and let me tell you both all about it."

Not really surprised that Cordelia was excited about what happened to her, as opposed to being upset or scared, Fiona followed along behind the siblings. She watched how tenderly Win walked with his hand on the small of his sister's back. Far from being the mean person she'd initially thought he was, he seemed to be a genuinely caring man.

The conductor met them before they got to the Barrington compartment. He greeted Cordelia. "I'm so glad you made it back aboard, Mrs. Barrington. I hope all is well with your arm."

"It's broken but I'll be fine. Thank you for your concern and thanks for making arrangements for me to get back to the train." She looked down at her clothing. "I hate to lose this dress as it was one of my favorites but since I'm still alive, I won't complain about the rips."

"We're glad to have you back on board. We couldn't very well keep you apart from your husband, now could we?" The man smiled at Cordelia. "I'm sure we can replace the dress for you."

"Thank you again for all your assistance." Win nodded at the conductor. "I'm hoping she will rest a bit now. Thank you for the offer on her clothing but we can replace it ourselves."

"We can talk about that later, sir. For now, I'll have your steward bring some warm towels. That seems to help the sore muscles." The conductor bowed and moved past them.

Upon reaching their compartment, Win unlocked the door and they all entered. Win led his sister to the sofa and, when she sat down, he pulled a blanket off the rack above it to place over her knees.

Cordelia giggled. "You're making me nervous, Barry."

He sat beside her. "Why's that?"

"When you're nice to me, it makes me think the world is going to end."

"Cordelia, he's been worried to death about you. You'd be surprised how frantic he's been to make sure you're all right." Fiona could scarcely believe that the girl was going to be such a tease to her brother, when all he'd wanted to do was make sure she was taken care of and on the way to recovery.

"Oh, never mind all that, Fi. I think he was only worried because he thought my mother would kill him if he lost me or if I was injured so badly that I couldn't be fixed. He's just relieved that I'm in one piece and he doesn't have to face the dragon-mother in her sitting room. That's where she always does the dressing-down of us sinners, right, Barry." Cordelia laughed and patted the seat beside her. "Come. Sit. Let me tell you all about my journey off the train."

"You *do* know that I tried to follow you, don't you? I attempted to catch up to you but got stopped by that Rozzelle man."

"What? You followed me? Really? I thought you said you didn't want to be part of the whole thing."

"I didn't but I couldn't very well let you roam around trying to solve Lucien's murder all on your own."

"Wait just a second." Win held up his hand. "What did Rozzelle do to you, Fiona?"

"Hey, this is my story, Barry. Why are you asking Fi about that old goat anyway? He's a jerk and I'm sure he didn't hurt her." Cordelia waved her hand in Fiona's direction. "See? She's fine."

"Hang on a sec, Cordelia. I want to know. It may be important."

"Lord. Why does your mission have to take priority over everything? Even your sister—oops, I mean wife?" Cordelia pouted for a second, then a smile brightened her face, "Who knows? What happened to me may be something that helps you solve whatever you're on board to solve."

Fiona looked from Win to Cordelia. "Solve? What's that mean?"

Cordelia slapped her hand over her mouth. "Oops. Sorry, Barry. I didn't mean to spill the beans on that."

Win glared at his sister. "You can't keep any secrets, can you? I should've known better than to bring you onboard with me."

Cordelia gasped. "You've known me a long time. What made you even dream that you could control me?"

"My mistake, for sure." Win stood and paced the small area between the benches.

"I guess you've been the soul of discretion even if you *were* worried about me." Cordelia's voice dripped sarcasm.

"Not quite. He's already spilled some information that he shouldn't. He told me that you're his sister, not his wife."

"*What?* Why would you do such a thing, Barry? Isn't it imperative that no one know that? If I told someone, you'd be ready to scalp me. Why can you blab it? Why would you trust her with our secret?"

He shrugged. "I don't really know. It just came out. I was frantic with worry about you and before I knew it, I'd spilled it."

"Some spy you are."

"Spy?" Fiona asked.

Cordelia slapped her hand up against her mouth again. "Oops. You didn't tell her *that* part? What story did you come up with then to explain why you'd pretend your sister is your wife? What could you have said that didn't sound perverted?"

"Never mind. I still want to hear about Rozzelle with Fiona and also about your ordeal." Win pulled out his notepad. "Let's start with how you got off the train and how you got injured."

"I thought you'd never ask." Cordelia grinned. She patted the seat beside her again. "Come sit back down so I can tell you all about it."

☙❧☙

Win sat and stared at his sister. She didn't seem like she'd been harmed other than the scrapes and the broken arm but he wasn't sure if she was mentally all right. True, she was acting normal but how would this affect her in the long term? She'd always been high strung and once the novelty of her so-called adventure wore off, she might have a breakdown.

He certainly hoped not. He wasn't sure he could handle Cordelia in full breakdown mode. He barely could handle her in full manic-mode, which she appeared to be in at the moment. He pulled his thoughts away from his worries about his sister and picked up the thread of the conversation she was having with Fiona.

"Like I said, I was shocked—utterly shocked—at the number of people back there."

"Back where?" Win asked.

"Are you paying any attention at all, Barry?"

"Yes, of course."

Cordelia shook her head at Fiona. "Men. He's clearly not heard a word I've said. If he had, he'd know back where, wouldn't he?"

Fiona smiled in Win's direction. "I think he would."

"All right. I confess, I was thinking about your injuries and not listening to your story. Forgive me?"

Fiona giggled. "That's sweet, Cordelia. You *have* to forgive him, don't you?"

"You're too easily swayed, Fi. Barry preys on the all the women at home with his charm and they let him get away with everything. Don't be like them. Help me teach him he needs to pay attention to women when they speak. He really never does, you know."

"Will you get on with your story and leave poor Fiona alone? She doesn't want to hear your nonsense about me. What happened to you?"

"Like I was telling Fi, I went through the second class compartments and eventually to an area of the train where there were several people gathered together in a circle. There were about eight of them and two of them were women. Or at least I think they were."

"How could you not know if they were women?" Fiona asked.

"They both had their backs to me and one wore a hooded cape. All I could see was part of her arm. She had it draped over a man's shoulder. I could see the forearm and a bracelet. I have to admit, the arm was kind of hairy, but there was that silver bracelet. You know?" Cordelia tilted her head at Win. "I mean, it seemed like a woman's bracelet, anyway."

"Would you recognize it again?" He asked.

"I think so."

Fiona leaned over and tapped Cordelia's knee. "That's good. Did she have anything to do with you going off the train?"

"Oh, I'm not sure. See, I walked in on them and they all looked so startled, I'm not even sure what happened. It was all kind of a blur. Just sensations, you know."

"How so?" Confused, Win wished Cordelia would get on with it. She was always so tedious when she was telling a story.

"It all happened so fast. One second I was there kneeling to pick up something, the light from the corridor shone on as I came in, and the next second several people were gaping at me in shock. Before I knew it, three of the men grabbed me, slid open the loading door, and out I went."

"Oh, my God." Fiona slapped her hand up against her mouth in stunned disbelief. "They tossed you off? Just like that?"

"Not before I picked up the shiny thing." Cordelia reached in her pocket. "I have it right here."

Win leaned forward. "What is it?"

"A mint. Look. It was wrapped in this paper that's kind of iridescent." Cordelia held it up toward Win.

His head spun. He recognized the mint as one of the ones that Jacques Cassel was constantly unwrapping and eating but how could that be? The man had been with him and that Perry man was playing cards. When would he have had a chance to throw Cordelia off the train? He did take a break to go to the lavatory. Would that have been enough time to get to that end of the train and back? Or was the wrapper there from earlier?

"What else did you notice? In the area?" Win asked Cordelia. He couldn't fathom how the candy wrapper got there but he was going to figure it out.

"It was really dark in that space but I could see that they were inspecting some kind of packages. Shaped a bit like bricks. You know—rectangular—but not quite as big as bricks." Cordelia held her hands apart a few inches to show them the size. "What do you think they might be, Barry?"

He didn't want to tell her what he thought, since he was sure she wouldn't be able to keep quiet about it. She might be in a lot more trouble anyway, once these people found out she was back on the train and maybe could identify them. This was not good. Not good at all. She was still in danger. Maybe even more now since they could get their hands on her again. Something told him they wouldn't fail to get rid of her the second time around.

He stayed silent a beat too long and she asked again, "Well? What do you think it was?"

Win shrugged. "I don't know, Cordelia. It could be anything really."

Cordelia bounced a little in her seat. "Personally, I think it could be drugs or maybe bars of gold."

"Surely not. You don't really think that could be it, do you?" Fiona asked in a breathless whisper.

"Look, you two need to stop speculating. This could be a problem." Win stood again and paced the small area. "These people didn't like you seeing what they were doing, Cordelia. They tossed you off the train. It's clear they have no concern whatsoever about your life or your safety. You have to be discreet. If you try to interfere with them or bring down the wrath of the authorities on them, they could very well kill you next time."

"But we need to figure out who killed Lucien," Cordelia protested.

"No, *we* don't. That's not why we're on this train."

"What if his death is related to whatever you're doing here?" Fiona asked. "Don't you have an obligation to at least *try* to figure that out?"

Win sat on the edge of the seat. "I think you're right but I want the two of you to stay out of this. I can work much better if I know you're both safe." He glanced over at Cordelia. "Can you promise me that you'll stay out of it?"

"You know I could promise you, Barry, and I'd have the best of intentions while I was doing so. You also know me well enough to be sure that I can be led astray in a moment. I hate to make a promise that I'm pretty sure I can't keep. I'm sorry but that's the way I am."

She was right. Much as he loved his sister, she was definitely right. He sometimes wondered how they came from the same family tree since they were so different.

"I worry about you, Cordelia." Win turned to Fiona. "And I want you to keep safe as well. You have to be fully aware each moment of where you are and who's around you."

"I think I can take care of myself. No one even knows I have anything to do with Cordelia and you other than sharing a table in the dining car." Fiona stood. "I think I need to head back to my compartment anyway. I have a book to read to make notes for my presentation in Istanbul and, besides, I'm tired from not sleeping much last night when I was worried about Cordelia."

"I'm so sorry you lost sleep over me, Fi."

"Before she leaves, can you tell us who else you saw back there in the circle of people? It may be important since Fiona may need to avoid them."

"Like I said, there was a second woman but I don't know who she was either. All I could see of her was her legs and shoes."

"Why was that all you could see?" Fiona asked.

"She was seated in the shadows and had her legs out in front of her crossed at the ankles. I could see she had on a brown tweed skirt, stockings, and some tan low-heeled shoes. That was all. I'd be able to recognize the shoes again, I'm sure. They were darling."

"Were any of the men any that you'd seen in the corridors, or the lounge, or maybe the dining car?" Win had his notebook out.

"Maybe." Cordelia nodded. "Like I said, it was pretty dark. I'll have to try to concentrate and remember. I really am tired now though and would like nothing better than to clean up and take a nap."

Fiona opened the door to the compartment. "I'll see you later, then. Get some rest. I'm going to try to do the same. Before I left home, I dreamed about riding on the train and staring out the window at the scenery and I haven't had a chance to do that yet."

"Look out there now." Cordelia pointed out the large window.

A beautiful cloud-filled sky hung over a field with a handmade fence. A small road meandered off to the side of the field.

"That's a wonderful view. I think I'll go to my compartment and dream of a knight in shining armor riding around the next corner. See you soon."

"Dream up one for me, too, Fi. Once I get rid of Barry, I'll need one."

Fiona laughed and turned to Win. "I guess she's really tired of being married to you, you poor dear."

"Not as tired as I am of her." Win grinned and took Fiona by the elbow. "May I escort you to your compartment?"

"If you think it's safe to leave Cordelia alone."

"She's never been one that it's safe to leave alone, but I think she can manage for ten minutes." He paused and pressed his thumb to the side of his nose as he looked over at Cordelia. "Right, sweetheart?"

Cordelia raised her eyebrows. "I'll try."

Win and Fiona stepped out of the compartment. Win made sure the door was locked before they headed down the corridor, even though he knew that if Cordelia decided to leave, she would do so without regard to what they'd discussed.

# Chapter 9

*Anger is a short madness. ~ Horace, Roman Poet, 65 BC-27 AD*

Fiona sat beside the window, lost in thought, until time to dress for dinner. She wasn't sure exactly what to think about Cordelia and her adventure. The woman sure was brave for someone Fiona thought of as spoiled and overprotected. It was admirable of her to survive that push off the train and still want to come back onboard, knowing that the very person who tossed her off would still be around and maybe try again. Or maybe try something much worse.

Fiona couldn't decide if the woman was crazy or not. She was pretty sure that she herself would've taken the first transport back to the safety of home. As she slipped on her second new dinner gown, she thought about all that had transpired since she boarded the train in Paris. This trip she won was certainly turning into much more than she bargained for. A murder, a friend tossed off the train and into the countryside, that scary man Johnny Rozzelle who she was sure was a member of the mafia, and then there was Win. Handsome Winchester Barrington, IV. Fiona let out a sigh as she slid the gown over her hips. He was really quite spectacular, even though she knew he was out of her reach.

A man of Win's background would have no use for a lowly librarian from the English countryside. She straightened her spine. So what? She could enjoy the time she had on the train and her conversations with him. Once she returned home, she could pine away for what could never be. *Buck up, old girl, and savor the time you do have with him. You'll need something to keep you warm this winter and those memories can go a long way toward that.*

Fiona pulled her hair up in a twist securing it with a crystal barrette. She sighed a little as she compared her fake accessories with the real diamond ones the other ladies in the first class coaches were going to be draped in at dinner. She made a face at herself in the mirror, shrugged, and mimicked her mother's voice, "Don't be getting above your station, luvvie. It'll lead to heartache."

Mother did sometimes know best and this time, Fiona knew, was no exception. The man was merely a dream for a short time in her life. With one last look at the mirror, Fiona smoothed an errant piece of hair down and, picking up her shawl and key, walked out of her compartment and straight into Win himself.

"Whoa, there, Fiona. Where are you going in such a hurry?"

"I'm sorry."

She glanced at him. He was magnificent in his tuxedo. Her knees buckled a little but she tightened them before she tipped forward. Of course, he looked amazing in the tux. He was born to wear one. Not like her and her awkwardness in formalwear.

"So, where are you headed?" Win asked again.

"To the dining car. Aren't you going the wrong way yourself? You seem to be dressed for the meal."

"Cordelia and I decided I needed to come escort you." He bowed. "Will you allow me to accompany you?"

"How is Cordelia getting there if you're here with me?" Fiona had to admit that her heart fluttered a bit at the thought of placing her arm in the crook of his elbow and allowing him to be her escort.

"I already dropped her off there and she's having a pre-dinner drink with Lady Marchman."

"Good. I was afraid you'd left her alone with Rozzelle or someone just as bad or worse."

"First of all, I'd never—"

"What are you saying about me?" Johnny Rozzelle asked, strolling into view.

Fiona gaped at him. *Oh Lord, now what?* He'd already been such a creep and now he'd heard her talking about him. She clenched her feet in her shoes, ready to run.

Win took Fiona by the elbow and squeezed it. "The lady was asking if you'd been moved from our dining table or if you would be joining us again."

"I did change tables but it wasn't because you requested it, Barrington. I changed to sit with a couple of other Americans. Ones who don't think they're too good for anyone but themselves. Have you met Mr. and Mrs. Donald and Abigail Perry?"

"I haven't had the pleasure," Win said.

"I met them briefly, I think," said Fiona. "He's a tall man who talks loud and she's a small woman who speaks so softly that she can't be heard, right?"

Rozzelle threw his head back and laughed. "You described them perfectly. The little Perry lady needs some attention I think. Her husband walks all over her. He has no idea of the caged lioness she really is." He smirked and winked broadly at Win. "You know what I mean, I bet." He patted Fiona on top of the head. "You, my dear, would have no clue, I'm afraid. It's too bad because you're quite the looker. It's a shame that you're so prudish."

Fiona gasped and jerked away from his hand. Her

hair fell out of its bun. She caught the barrette before it hit the floor. "You're disgusting. Keep your hands off me."

Win took a step forward as if to punch the other man. "Look here, Rozzelle, that's no way to behave with a lady present. Leave her be."

Fiona pulled on Win's arm. "Stop. Let him go by. He's a waste of time."

"Speaking of wastes of time, Barrington, I don't know what you see in this little mouse when you have that nice, vibrant piece in your own compartment. How is the little wife anyway?" Rozzelle kept the smirk firmly in place as he taunted Win.

Win punched Rozzelle in the face. "Shut the hell up."

Rozzelle shoved Win up against the wall of compartment and held him there by the upper arms. "Don't you ever touch me again. You will more than regret it. You have two ladies on this train you seem to care about, and if you make one more move against me, you'll lose at least one of them, if not both." He shoved back on Win once more and then let go. The he turned to Fiona and bowed. "Better keep your boyfriend in line, missy, if you don't want to pick up the pieces I leave when I'm done with him."

He spun on his heel and headed toward the dining car.

Fiona, her hands shaking, turned to Win. "Are you all right? He was a bit rough, wasn't he?"

"I'm fine." Win pushed his hair off his face and glanced down at Fiona. "He's messed up your hairdo. Let's go back inside and fix it."

"I can do that. You need to get to the dining car and check on Cordelia since that odious man is going that way. I'm worried about her."

"She'll be fine. There was already a crowd there and I'm certainly not leaving you alone with that gorilla on the loose. Come." He reached for Fiona's hand. "Give me your key and we'll see to your hair quickly."

She handed him the key and he opened her door. She stepped in past him and over to the mirror. He picked up the hairbrush she'd left nearby.

"May I?"

Confused, she stared up at him.

He twirled his finger in the air. "Turn around."

She faced the mirror and he ran the brush through her hair. No man had ever done that for her before and she lost her balance. Falling against him, she hit his broad chest with her shoulder blades.

He steadied her with his hands. Their warmth invaded her body and the blood pooled in her stomach. This was not good. Her attraction to him was growing and she knew she had to resist.

His voice gruff, he said, "Where's your clip?"

"My clip?"

"The thing you had in your hair?"

"Oh." She was so distracted, she couldn't think. Feeling foolish, she handed it to him over her shoulder.

Win took it from her and clipped her hair back into its bun. "That looks fine. I think."

Fiona turned her head to the side to look. "It does. How did you learn to make twists?"

"Remember how bossy my sister can be?"

Fiona laughed. "Yes. I guess she made you play with her?"

"She did."

He smiled at Fiona in the mirror. His grin almost knocked her to her knees. No man should be allowed to be so handsome. His kindness to his sister also endeared him to Fiona.

She cleared her throat. "I think we better go to the dining car."

"You're right."

Taking the brush from his hand, Fiona placed it on the counter and turned to the door.

Win stepped behind her and planted a small kiss on the nape of her neck.

She shuddered and he pulled her against his chest, whispering in her ear, "You are beautiful, Fiona Vancleave and don't let anyone tell you otherwise."

She wanted to stay in his arms forever but she knew he was only trying to make her feel better after what Rozzelle said. Wouldn't it be wonderful if he really

thought she was beautiful and wanted to be with her? Too
bad that was merely part of the dream that would have to
entertain her by the fireside this winter.

ℰↁℰↁ

They left Fiona's compartment and moved toward
the dining car. Win did his best to hide the way he react-
ed to her. He didn't think she'd noticed in her cabin how
she affected him. He berated himself for giving in even
for a moment to the lust he experienced when she was
around. Her fresh scent of lemon verbena and her smile
was enough to send him into overdrive. He should never
have picked up her hairbrush and touched her hair. What
folly that was.

He was a bit surprised at his control. He wanted the
woman so badly but knew she wasn't someone to be tak-
en lightly. He surely couldn't afford the distraction she
would be—hell, who was he kidding?—she already was a
distraction. He had to get his head back into his mission.
He couldn't afford this complication. At all. He had to be
successful in his quest and he had to teach Rozzelle a lesson. The man was a pig when it came to women and he
needed a thrashing.

Fiona's hand on his forearm as they made their way
down the corridor made it hard to concentrate. What was
he going to do? How could he get her out of his mind?

"What's that fierce look about?"

He glanced down at her as she strolled along beside him. "What?"

"Your expression is quite frightening. It's almost as bad as the one you wore the first moment I met you."

Win couldn't help but laugh. "That bad, huh?"

"Terrifying." She shuddered. "I much prefer that you save that one for Rozzelle and his ilk."

"Or for Cordelia when I'm especially angry at her?"

"For sure." Fiona's laughter echoed down the hallway as he opened the door to the dining car.

Mack Plant grabbed the door from Win and held it open. "What's so funny?"

"Nothing. Miss Vancleave was making fun of the way I look at my wife when she's particularly trying." Win shook Plant's hand. "How are you this evening?"

"I was hoping to catch up with you."

Win frowned. "What's up?"

He wasn't sure what Plant needed but he didn't want the cop talking about Lucien's death in front of Fiona. It was going to be a detailed conversation and he didn't know how squeamish she would be about autopsy results. Although the man *had* died on her lap.

"I heard that the chap called Rozzelle who was seated at your table last night has been moved to mine. I was wondering if you'd take pity on a Chicago cop and let me sit with you since you now have an empty seat."

"Do you not want to sit with him since he's mafia? Is he part of Capone's gang?" Fiona asked.

Plant gaped at her. "What?"

"Is he mafia? You said you're a Chicago policeman, didn't you? Wasn't Capone in your city before he went to prison? Wouldn't you know some of his gang?"

Win patted Fiona's arm. "Shh. It's not safe to ask such questions too loudly."

"I have no idea about Johnny Rozzelle but I would be interested in hearing your theory." Plant shook his head. "Over at the table, though, not here in the doorway."

Win grinned at Plant. "Then I guess you're invited to eat with us."

"It's only fair that the lovely lady have a single man to entertain her since you're married to the equally ravishing Cordelia."

Win wanted nothing more than to let the man know that he was not going to let Fiona be entertained in any way other than at dinner. Shocked at how much he didn't want Plant to flirt with Fiona, Win glanced around the dining room to see who was present.

Cordelia waved at him across the room. He headed in her direction with Fiona and Mack in his wake.

When they arrived at the table, Win made a show of kissing Cordelia on the cheek. "How are you, darling?" He sat beside her.

"Lovely now that my handsome husband has joined me." Cordelia glanced up at Fiona. "Come and sit, my friend. I think I'm going to have to order something that I don't need to cut." She lifted her arm in the sling. "I'm not going to be able to use a knife for sure."

Win smiled at Cordelia and patted her good hand that rested on the table. "Darling, you know I'll cut your steak for you."

"Good because I was craving a T-bone so much." Cordelia smiled over at Mack as he and Fiona took their seats across from the Barringtons. "What kind of meat do you like, Mr. Plant?"

"I'm a carnivore connoisseur, Mrs. Barrington. I'll eat any meat that comes along."

"Please, Mr. Plant, call me Cordelia. My mother— ahem, mother-in-law—is Mrs. Barrington."

Fiona let out a little gasp. Win stepped on her toe under the table and shook his head. Good Lord, one of these women was going to give away the game, and soon, if he didn't watch out.

He should have known better than to let a good-looking man like Plant get near Cordelia. She was a hopeless flirt. Always had been.

"Then you must call me Mack."

Cordelia nodded at Fiona. "I shall. It's such a manly name, isn't it, Fi?"

Fiona smiled at the man seated beside her. "It sure is and, not only that, he's a macho cop from Chicago."

"Darling, please stop flirting with the man. You sometimes seem to forget that I'm here and can be quite the jealous husband." Win gritted his teeth. Cordelia needed to stick to the plan and stop her incessant come-ons to other men.

"Oh, dear, you know you're the only man for me." Cordelia looked over at Mack. "At least for this week, Mr. Plant."

It was all Win could do to maintain his decorum. This chit was going to have to be locked in her compartment, if she wasn't going to blow their cover.

Mack winked at her. "Then, I'll wait for next week before I ask you out to the theatre."

A small foot stepped on Win's toe before he could respond. He knew his face had to be red since he sensed his blood pressure rise.

Fiona laughed. "You're so funny, Mr. Plant. Anyone can see they were meant for each other. I'm quite sure Cordelia is teasing her husband."

Thank God for Fiona. She was a gem to try to cover for Cordelia and stop him from killing his own sister.

"I have no doubt that she is teasing him because she can get a rise out of him," Mack said. He patted Fiona's arm. "I've seen married couples like them a lot in my work. They bait each other in public and then the passion flares in private. It's kind of a game to them. Keeps them each on their toes."

Fiona smiled across the table at the Barringtons. "I find it kind of odd but I can see what you mean."

Relieved that Mack seemed fooled, Win picked up his menu. "Let's see what's being served this evening."

Cordelia batted her eyelashes at Win. "Ooh, look, darling. It's *coq a vin*. One of my favorites. Let's order a nice chardonnay to go with it."

Great. Now she was going to go overboard the other way and fawn over him. Torn over the way he wanted her to behave and not getting satisfaction from anything she did, Win hoped the dinner would pass quickly and uneventfully.

"Sure. Chardonnay would go well with it." he glanced over at Mack and Fiona. "I'll order two bottles. All right?"

"That would be lovely, Mr. Barrington," Fiona said.

"Please, call me Win."

Cordelia batted her eyelashes again. "Why are you having her call you Win, Barry? Don't all your friends call you Barry?"

He really was going to kill her before the evening was over—or maybe just strangle her slightly. "No, dear, they don't. My pals from school do and you do but most everyone else calls me Win. Even my mother calls me Win."

Cordelia smiled. "Well, it would hardly be appropriate for her to call you Barry, would it? She calls your father Chester, doesn't she?"

"She does. It's the curse of being the fourth person with the same name. Granddad is called Winchester, dad is Chester, and I'm Win. Thank goodness all four of us weren't alive at the same time. No telling how the names would've ended up." Win glanced up as the sommelier appeared and ordered the two bottles of wine.

Once the sommelier was gone, Fiona asked, "So, will you name your son Winchester the fifth?"

Cordelia shuddered. "I imagine he will have to. Dad—Barry's father—would probably die from a heart attack if he didn't."

"I can see that they'd want to keep up the tradition since it's gone on so long. What's the reason for the first Winchester or is it an old family name that got revived?" Mack asked.

"Actually, it's a wonderful story. Barry's great grandfather was rescued from a sure death, by Mr. Oliver Winchester. You know, the man who invented the repeating rifle? It was during the French and Indian wars that he saved the great grandfather's life on the battlefield. Granddad named his first born in honor of Mr. Winchester and the tradition has continued." Cordelia tapped the table with her index finger. "I'm hoping for girls so the name can be dropped."

Win snickered. He couldn't resist saying what came to mind. "Oh, no darling, if I sire a girl, she shall be named Winnie. Winnie Fred Barrington."

Cordelia slapped his arm as Fiona and Mack burst into laughter.

Fiona was the first to recover. "Not even Winifred?"

"Nope." Win shook his head. "Two names. Winnie and Fred."

Cordelia groaned and put her head in her one good hand. "I can't stand it."

"Good enough reason for a divorce in my opinion," Mack said.

"Thank you. I may have to do that." Cordelia looked over at Mack. "Since you're a cop, could I hire you to be my investigator to catch Barry in some kind of compromising position—maybe with my friend, Fi here—so I'd have the grounds for the divorce?"

Mack opened his mouth to answer but Fiona spoke first. "Oh no, Cordelia. I can't be named as a third party in a divorce."

Win kicked the side of his sister's shin. She had to stop this nonsense. He noticed the red flush of Fiona's face and the way her neck also reddened. His mind went where he'd tried not to go. He pictured her in his arms with his lips on her cleavage that was so appealing at the moment. He could imagine the way she would pant in the throes of making love and how the flush of lust would cover her chest.

"Are you all right?" Mack asked Win. "I figured you'd have some comment to make with your wife being so provocative and there you sit as if you were struck dumb."

"I just can't believe that the woman I married would be so crass as to have such a discussion at the dinner table. I happen to know she was raised better than that."

Cordelia winked. "Ah, Barry. See, that's one of the

problems we have with our marriage. You don't appreciate my sense of humor."

"I certainly don't, especially when it's at the expense
of someone who has been as kind to you as Fiona has."

"I didn't really mean I wanted to tarnish Fi's reputation. I was teasing."

"You should watch how you tease. I think you got
her upset." Win made eye contact with Fiona. "Right?"

Fiona ducked her head. "It was a little unsettling but
since Cordelia said she was kidding, it's all right."

"Let's change the subject and talk about something
more entertaining than divorce cases," Mack suggested.

Grateful for the suggestion, Win said, "Yes. There
has to be something else more amusing."

"I hear there's a new theatre in Constantinople. Let's
plan a night out there when we get to the city," Cordelia
said.

"You mean Istanbul, Cordelia. How could you forget
that they changed the name?" Win asked.

"Never mind the history lesson, darling. What about
the theatre?"

"That would be lovely. I'd like that," Fiona said.

Mack smiled as the waiter arrived at the table to
bring their meals. "Then let's do it."

# Chapter 10

Friendship often ends in love; but love in friendship, never. ~ *Charles Caleb Colton, British Clergyman, 1780-1832*

Once the interminable meal was over, Fiona excused herself and headed outside to get a breath of fresh air. Every time she looked up, it seemed Win turned his head as if he'd been caught staring at her. It rattled her equilibrium. She had to get away to regain her composure. She darted through the lounge area where several of the first class passengers had gathered for after dinner drinks.

Standing on the little sheltered platform at the back of the lounge car, she took in several deep breaths.

A few curls escaped from her up-do and tickled her cheek. She shoved the offenders behind her right ear. That action reminded her of the intimate act of Win fixing her hair. That, combined with his kiss on her neck, had sent her reeling and she could barely concentrate during the walk down the corridor to the dining car.

When Cordelia suggested that she wanted to use her as the reason for her fake divorce, Fiona had glanced up at Win and the look on his face made her wonder if he really could be interested in her.

He quickly berated his sister for her words and then didn't really make eye contact again with Fiona during the rest of the meal. That must mean she was imagining that glint in his eye.

Oh, would that the man *could* want her. He was so handsome with the air of mystery about him. And why he was on the train, pretending to be married to his sister, only added to his appeal. She shook herself. *Get a grip. You're being silly over someone who has zero interest in you.*

"Are you cold?"

The voice startled her and Fiona let out a little scream. She whirled around. "*Monsieur* Cassel, you startled me."

"I meant no harm, lovely lady. You seemed to be shivering and I was going to offer you the use of my coat." Jacques Cassel fingered the edge of his suit lapel. "Do you need it?"

"No thank you. I wasn't really cold although the wind seems to be picking up now. Will you excuse me while I return to the lounge?"

"If you will allow me to treat you to a drink from the bar." He held the door open to allow her to pass.

She shook her head. "That's not necessary."

Why would he want to have a drink with her? Had he followed her outside on purpose?

"Please. I must confess. I followed you out here because I wanted to talk to you for a moment. Would that be acceptable? It won't take long."

Fiona stepped past him and into the lounge. Over her shoulder, she said, "I only have time for one drink since I have some paperwork to do in my compartment."

Curious as to why he wanted to speak to her, she was still leery because of Cordelia's earlier statement about the mint candy wrappers and the one she had picked up at the back of the train and still had in her pocket.

Fiona supposed it would be better to have whatever discussion the man wanted to have with witnesses present. If he were the one who threw Cordelia off the train, it would at least be safer inside the lounge than on the outer platform.

Cassel snapped his fingers at the waiter. "What will you have?"

"Gin and tonic please."

He looked down his long, patrician nose at Fiona. "Ahh, of course, a very British choice."

Putting on her haughtiest expression, she pulled out a chair and sat at the closest table. "Nothing wrong with a good old G and T, is there?"

He held up both hands as if in surrender. "Far be it from me to question a beautiful lady on her choice of beverage."

The waiter appeared beside Cassel's elbow and took their orders. As soon as the man was out of hearing, Fiona leaned forward. "What can I do for you?"

"I wondered about the health of your friend, Mrs. Barrington." Cassel pulled a peppermint from his jacket pocket and rattled the paper as he opened it. He placed it on his tongue as he awaited her response.

Fiona's gut clenched at his words. Was he going to threaten her? Was he the one who threw Cordelia off the train? Did he know her friend had picked up his misplaced candy? She glanced around at the others drinking in the area.

No one was paying any attention to her and the Frenchman. She didn't know if that was a good thing or not.

"Miss Vancleave?"

She looked into his eyes. "Yes."

"How is your friend?"

"She's fine. Of course, she has a broken arm and some scrapes but overall, she's well."

"I'm glad to hear that. I was concerned to hear she'd gone off the train while it was still in motion. Tell me, did she say how it happened?" Cassel unwrapped another mint and popped it in his mouth.

Their drinks arrived. Fiona took a large swig of hers before she answered. She used the time to formulate a bland response. The man was definitely pumping her for information.

Once she swallowed, she said, "Cordelia didn't know. She said it was dark back where she was and the next thing she knew, she was rolling down an embankment."

"Hmm." Cassel scratched his chin. "That was all she recalled?"

"That's it. To tell you the truth, I think she hit her head, and has a bit of amnesia because of what happened. She really had no idea how she got off the train. She didn't see anyone and she woke up in a hospital. Apparently the fall knocked her out for a while."

Fiona hoped the mixture of truth and lies would help protect her friend. Cassel seemed overly intent on finding out how much Cordelia knew about what had happened. Maybe he was afraid she could identify him as being involved.

"It would seem to me that if she were having amnesia, she couldn't be perfectly fine as you indicated you think she is."

"Oh well, you know, she *is* all right physically but she can't really say how it happened. She can't recall any specific detail is what she said. She also said the doctor suspected a concussion." Fiona darted a glance around the room again and noticed Win seated at a table with Hugh Marchman and that American man she thought he called Perry. Win focused on her and Cassel. He seemed to be ignoring his companions as he stared across the space between the tables. The heat of his stare made her both uncomfortable and comfortable. Uncomfortable since he was so intent but it was also comforting to know someone was paying attention in case the Frenchman tried something.

"I sure would like to talk to her about it. Do you think she'd discuss it with me?" Cassel asked.

Fiona shrugged. "I'm sure I don't have an answer to that question. I also know Cordelia well enough to suspect that she would want to know why you think it's any concern of yours."

"Can we merely say it's my own curiosity?"

"You can try but I don't think Cordelia will buy it. If you're going to have a conversation with her about it, I suggest that you come up with a better reason than that. That is if you want to get any information from her."

He leaned back and eyed her in a way that caused her blood to freeze. "Is that what you think I'm doing? Gathering information?"

"It sure appears to be what you're doing." Fiona drained her glass and stood. "Now, if you'll excuse me, I need to get to work on polishing my presentation I'm to give in Istanbul."

Cassel stood and bowed. "Thank you for your time."

"Thank you for the drink." She walked away from the table and toward the door that led to the corridor.

Before she could make good on her escape, Lady Sarah Marchman hailed her from a table near the door. "Fiona, come over and meet my friend."

Fiona sighed. She'd already met the woman seated with Lady Sarah. It was the mousy wife of that Perry man that she'd ran into in the corridor. The man who asked her if her last name was German.

She couldn't recall the lady's name at the moment and hoped Lady Sarah would provide it. Arriving at the table, Fiona said, "I'm on my way to my compartment to work on my presentation."

"Oh, dear. It's like being with my husband. He's always working on his lectures." Lady Sarah turned to the Perry woman. "Is your husband like that, Abigail?"

The other woman shook her head. "No. My husband isn't an intellectual at all. He's more the hands-on kind of man. He owns mills and all. He's interested in is the production of wools and blends and how much he can sell. I'm not sure he's even *read* a book in the last five years, much less written a lecture or presentation." Abigail tittered nervously as she glanced over at her husband seated with Win.

Lady Sarah patted the seat next to her. "Sit with us a few moments, Fiona. Surely your work can wait a little while."

Not wanting to be rude, Fiona sat. "What did you want to talk to me about?"

"Let's get you a drink first." Lady Sarah moved her arm as if to wave at the waiter.

"No, thank you. I had some gin a moment ago and shared too much wine with my table-mates at dinner. If I'm going to get any work done, I need to stop with the liquor."

"Come on. One more won't hurt." Lady Sarah got the waiter's attention.

When he arrived, Fiona turned to him. "Nothing for me although my friend here seems to need a refill."

"Coming right up," the waiter said. He smiled at Abigail. "For you as well, Mrs. Perry?"

"Sure. I've got nothing better to do." Abigail let out another titter. The waiter smiled and left them alone.

"I don't know why you don't want another. It's not like you'd be drunk. You seem pretty sober," Lady Sarah said. She seemed to be pouting and Fiona was at a loss as to why the woman seemed to be pushing her to drink.

Why did she care so much if Fiona had one drink or twenty?

Fiona tapped her foot. "I prefer to decide for myself if I want a drink, not to have one foisted on me. Please let me know what you need so I can be on my way."

"Well, the little librarian has teeth, Abigail." Lady Sarah laughed, a nasally, unpleasant sound. "I didn't know you had it in you to be rude, Fiona. I have to say,

I'm not quite sure how I feel about this side of you. Maybe I've misjudged you."

"I have no idea why you'd be judging me in the first place, Lady Sarah, but I really don't care. After all, it's not like we move in the same circles and the chances of us meeting each other after this trip is over are slim to none." Fiona stood. "I think it's time for me to go."

"But we so wanted to hear how your friend Cordelia is. We saw her at dinner but didn't have a chance to speak to her. We noticed her arm was in a sling. Will she make a full recovery? Does she remember what happened?"

Lady Sarah's smile seemed false. Fiona couldn't help but wonder why everyone seemed to be so concerned about Cordelia and what she might recall, but no one wanted to ask the lady herself. Why did they all think Fiona was the proper person to ask?

"I think you'd be better off asking her yourself. I know she didn't feel up to a long conversation tonight and that her arm was causing her some pain. I imagine she's back in her compartment, taking it easy for the rest of the evening." Fiona turned to walk away but before she left, she added, "I see her husband seated over there. Why not ask him how she is? Please excuse me." She stalked out of the lounge.

As she made her way down the corridor, she couldn't help thinking about all the questions about Cordelia. She wondered which of the passengers who asked about her health were really concerned about her friend and which may have been involved in getting her off the train in the first place. Her head awhirl, she was startled when a hand took hold of her upper arm.

She whirled around. Relief washed over her at the realization that the person attached to the hand was Win. She'd been frightened for a moment that it was Rozzelle or maybe Cassel.

"Do you have a moment?" Win asked.

Fiona stopped in her tracks and looked up at him. "If I get asked that question one more time today, I shall go absolutely mad and jump off this train myself."

"Don't even kid about such as that." His grip on her arm tightened. "I don't want anyone thinking that's an option."

Fiona kept moving down the hall. "Are you always so literal?"

"No but when someone has already been pushed off, I don't think joking about it is a good idea. I'd hate to see anything else like that happen to anyone I know." He barked a laugh. "Or anyone I don't know for that matter."

"Me either and I really have no plans to take a dive out the door. Trust me on that." Arriving at her door, Fiona pulled her key out of her evening bag.

Win leaned his shoulder on the wall beside her. "Don't go in yet."

She turned toward him. "Why?"

He reached out and wrapped one of the curls hanging

down from her up-do around his index finger. He lifted it to his nose and sniffed.

"Lemon verbena. One of my favorite scents."

Fiona's legs trembled beneath her gown. Heat pooled in her loins. He was so handsome and his attentions made her toes curl in her shoes. She knew he was merely flirting with her because there was no one else on the train who knew he wasn't married, but she wanted it to mean something anyway.

"What did you want to talk to me about?" she asked.

"Why were you talking to Jacques Cassel? You know he could have been the one to throw Cordelia out that door and off the train. Why would you take a chance on chatting with him?"

"He followed me outside when I stepped out for some air. I tried to avoid him but he came inside right after me and asked me to have a drink. I didn't want to seem rude, so I had one with him. I moved away as quickly as I could and then got stopped by Lady Sarah."

He teased another curl that lay against her neck. His fingers brushed her collarbone. "I saw you chatting with the ladies. What was that about?"

She suppressed a shudder at his warm touch and tried to concentrate on the conversation. "They were also asking about Cordelia. It seems as if everyone wants to chat about Cordelia and her health but it seems odd that no one wants to ask the lady herself."

"I imagine it's on everyone's mind. They really

should be asking about poor Lucien but they seem to be more interested in my sister, don't they?"

"Yes. I find that odd as well."

Win's index finger slid down the side of Fiona's neck. He was really going to have to stop before she collapsed at his feet. It was almost too much for her to bear. She decided she needed to escape and placed her key in the lock.

"What have we here?" an American voice asked. It was Mack Plant.

Fiona turned around. "What do you mean?"

"I'm beginning to wonder about that conversation at dinner." Plant slapped Win on the back. "Are you out here trying to be caught in a delicate situation so your lovely wife can call for a divorce?"

"*What*?" Fiona gasped.

Mack waggled a finger at them. "This looks a lot like a tryst." He clapped a hand on Win's shoulder. "I confess, Barrington, that I'd love for your beautiful wife to be divorced. I'd pursue her myself if she were free."

Fiona's heart dropped. Good God, if Mr. Plant thought she and Win were having an affair and spoke of it, what would happen to her reputation? She couldn't have this. Not at all.

Before she could speak, Win said, "It's not a tryst, Plant. We're having a discussion about all the various people who've inquired about my wife to Miss Vancleave. I think one of them may be involved in her *adven-*

*ture* as she calls it and I was asking Fiona here about the conversations. Obviously, if we were having an illicit relationship, we'd hardly carry it on in the corridor, would we?"

"Still, it seems a bit suspicious, my friend, what with you fondling the lady's hairdo." Mack raised an eyebrow.

"On that note, I think I'll go to bed. I'd like to think you'll keep your thoughts about this matter to yourself, Mr. Plant," Fiona said.

Plant bowed. "Most certainly. A gentleman never tells, right?"

Fiona gave him a small smile and turned the key in the lock. She opened the door and entered her compartment.

As she shut the door, she heard Win say, "Come, Plant, let's go play a few hands of poker."

She hoped Win would find a way to keep the man from blabbing his suppositions all over the train.

❧❧❧

Win and Mack hadn't taken three steps before Win spotted Johnny Rozzelle at the end of the corridor chatting with the new steward who'd taken Lucien's place— or at least he presumed he was Lucien's replacement. Win let out a breath. He sure didn't want to talk to that oaf again, although he knew he had to since the man was one of his main suspects. It was just that the man was so obnoxious.

"What's with the sigh?" Mack asked.

"I don't care for Rozzelle at all. He's been incredibly rude to both my—uh, Cordelia—as well as Fiona."

"Ah, I like that."

Win glanced at Plant in shock. "What? That the man was rude to the ladies?"

"No. That you finally called Cordelia yours."

"I did what?"

"You said, 'my Cordelia.' I really was afraid you were going to throw over your beautiful wife for that nice, but hardly gorgeous, Miss Vancleave."

"What's wrong with Fiona's looks?"

They arrived at the end of the corridor. Mack reached for the door between the cars and, as he did, Rozzelle said, "Are you two arguing over the lovely, yet shy, Miss Vancleave? If so, I'd like to get my claim in as well. What do you think? Can we all share that pretty little piece of—"

Win slugged Rozzelle in the jaw. Rozzelle fell against the steward who held on to the shorter man. Win's fist rose for a second hit but Mack stopped him by grabbing Win's hand with his palm.

"Stop it, Barrington. There's no need in getting violent."

"You heard him disparage Miss Vancleave. We can't let him get away with that."

Rozzelle freed himself from the steward. "Look here, Barrington. You're out of control. What the hell makes you think you're the defender of that little lady? Don't you have a wife? What does she think about you wanting to defend some other chit's honor?" Rozzelle rubbed his chin. "I'm going to have to get my revenge you know. I can't let you walk around here attacking people for no cause."

"*No cause*? Did you really just say no cause?" Win knew he was in danger of losing it again and couldn't fathom why. He barely knew Fiona Vancleave. What the hell was he thinking to punch this man who would be a very dangerous enemy? He needed to get his head cleared and fast.

"I did indeed, Mr. Barrington. I am going back to my compartment now but I suggest you watch yourself and your beautiful wife for the remainder of this trip. Like I said, I don't take kindly to being assaulted." Rozzelle stalked away.

"Excuse us." Plant nodded at the steward and pulled Win through the door. "Come on. You need to cool off. I can't say that I understand you."

"I merely don't like men like that belittling women. Any women."

They walked on toward the lounge car. Plant stayed silent. Win stewed over Rozzelle. Inside the lounge, the two men sat at a table and Mack pulled out a deck of cards. "What game?"

"Five card stud?"

"Sure but we need a few more." Mack stood and glanced around the room. He called out, "Starting some stud poker over here. All comers welcome."

A few men joined them, including Donald Perry and Hugh Marchman. Donald stood behind Marchman's chair. Hugh turned to address Donald. "Come, join us. The evening is young."

"I really have to go. I made arrangements to meet with a man I met earlier on the trip. He may very well place an order with my company. If I sit at this table, I may lose money instead of making money."

He brayed like a mule and Win cringed inwardly. He wouldn't be sad about Perry refusing to play.

"Better be off with yourself then," Hugh said.

"I shall but first I'd like to ask Barrington a question."

Win made eye contact with the man over Hugh's head. "What's that?"

"That girl who's been hanging about with your wife—"

Win suppressed his anger. "What about her?"

How many more people had noticed Fiona around and were going to comment on it? Had Cordelia being friends with her compromised his investigation? Who was he kidding? He'd compromised himself by showing her special attention when he was supposed to be married.

"What do you know about her?"

"Not a whole lot. She's friendlier with my wife than me. I know she's a librarian from a small town in England. That's about all."

The man leaned his fist on the table and glared at Win. "Don't you think it's suspicious that she's on this train and in the first class section? How does she afford such as that?"

Taken aback a bit at the man's vehemence, Win didn't respond.

"What are you trying to say against the lady?" Mack asked.

"We all know how expensive this mode of transport is. How does she pay for it? *That's* my question." Donald paused a moment and looked at each man in turn. "What business does a young librarian have in Istanbul anyway?"

"It's my understanding from my *own* wife's conversations with the young lady that she won some type of contest and is going to be giving some kind of lecture about the train's history at the institute," Hugh said. "Now, let's play some cards. You go tend to your business and leave the poor girl alone."

"That's exactly my point. The *poor* girl." Donald sneered as he said the words.

Win was losing his temper and ready to throttle the man. Or at least tape his mouth shut so he'd go away and leave them alone. "Look, what are you hinting at here,

Perry? Come out and tell us all so we can get on with the game."

"No one here thinks it's odd that she has a German name?" Perry asked.

"Vancleave is German?" Mack asked.

Win slammed the deck of cards to the table. "Oh, good God, man, what are you implying?"

"I think the woman is a spy. A German spy. I say we expose her for what she is and get her off this train." Perry practically snarled the words.

"You *have* got to be kidding me." Win picked up the deck and handed it to Mack. "Shuffle and let's ignore this lout."

"How dare you call me a lout, sir." Donald's voice cracked on the last word.

"How dare *you* call a young girl a German spy? You're delusional if you think that unassuming, naïve woman works for Hitler," Win said.

"I think not. She's on this train to find information for Hitler and I'm going to prove it. You all will be admitting I'm right before we get to Istanbul." Perry turned on his heel and stomped out of the room.

As soon as he was gone, Mack dealt the cards. Win couldn't help but wonder why the American thought Fiona was a spy. Had he seen her behaving in an odd or secretive manner? Had she said something that could be interpreted as if she were gathering intelligence?

Could it be true that she was some agent for Hitler's

Nazi party? Win didn't want to think so because if she was, she was way more clever than he. She seemed to be so innocent and sweet. What if he was being played? Could she be that good? To fool him after all his training?

He shook his head to clear it and glanced down at his cards. As he looked at the hand he'd been dealt, it dawned on him suddenly that it was vitally important to his own happiness and wellbeing that Donald Perry was wrong about Fiona.

# Chapter 11

Waste no more time arguing what a good man should be. Be one. ~ *Marcus Aurelius, Roman Emperor, AD 121-180*

The morning sun, peeking around the bottom edge of the blind that wasn't drawn all the way down, woke Fiona early. She stretched her legs toward the end of the bunk and let out a contented sigh. She'd slept well, having finally gotten used to the clacking of the wheels on the tracks. When she used to visit her grandmother as a child, the first couple of nights were always sleepless as Fiona heard the grandfather clock song go off each fifteen minutes.

By the time she'd been at her grandmother's for a

couple of nights, her mind had blocked out those chimes. This was the same kind of thing and she was glad to finally be well rested.

Without taking off her blankets, she sat up and leaned forward. Lifting the edge of the blinds, she peered out at the passing landscape. There was a stream over a small ridge running alongside the tracks. She wondered how cold the water was. It sure looked pretty but she was sure it was probably icy cold.

A knock on the door startled her. She glanced at the little travel clock in the leather case, that her coworkers gave her when they learned she'd won the trip. It was only a few minutes after six and she hadn't ordered early coffee to be delivered. "Hold on a moment."

She tossed back the covers, slid on her robe that rested at the foot of the bed, and walked across to the door. Opening the door, she glanced around puzzled. There was no one there. The steward sat at the end of the corridor. Rather than call out to him and risk waking the others who had compartments in the car and were probably still asleep, Fiona stepped out into the hallway.

Her foot slipped on something. She looked down. She stood on an envelope with her name on the outside. "What's this?"

Fiona knelt and picked up the envelope. Opening it, she scanned the contents. Her blood ran cold. No signature.

She glanced back down the corridor at the steward.

Her mind made up, she strolled down to where he sat. When she arrived at his side, she asked, "Who left this outside my door?"

"I'm afraid I don't know, Miss Vancleave."

"How can you not know? Isn't this your post?"

"It is but I've only been on duty for a few minutes. We don't sit out here all night. We have an area where we can rest during the early hours of the morning, where we can hear the bell if called. Since most people are in their compartments asleep for those hours and have limited needs, the company doesn't have a steward out here for the entire night."

Fiona placed her hands on her hips. "The knock on my door happened a less then two minutes before I opened it. You can't tell me that there was such a crowd out here in the hallway that you have no idea who left this note."

"There were actually a couple of people out here in the last few minutes, mademoiselle. One was a lady in a white fur coat who asked for coffee and another was a man in a suit. He passed through. I didn't notice either of them at your door."

"Who were they?"

"I told you. A man in a suit and a woman in a white coat."

*"Please."* Fiona tapped her toe. "Don't try to put me off. We both know that the stewards as well as the waiters and other staff of the Wagons-Lit Company make it a

practice to know their passengers—especially the first class ones—by name. It's a point of pride for them to do so. I *know* you know exactly who was in this corridor and I want you to tell me. Now."

"Actually, Miss Vancleave, I'm still learning names since I took over when Lucien was killed so I'm not completely sure who they were."

"Give it a guess then. It's important."

"The man was the one who is always chewing on mints and leaving wrappers all over the place."

"That's Jacques Cassel."

"Yes." The steward nodded. "That's his name. Right."

"What about the woman?"

"She's going to be harder to describe."

"Why's that?" Fiona was nearing the end of her patience. This was taking too long. Her head spun as the back of her mind mulled over the contents of the letter. She needed to know who left it. She didn't know what to do about it but as soon as she got the information about the woman, she planned to dress and get some assistance from Win.

He was the only person on board that she thought she could trust to lead her in the right direction. Maybe that Mack who was a cop could help her but she wasn't sure about him.

"She was wearing a black scarf over her face—"

"*What*? She was dressed like some kind of western

train robber with a scarf over her mouth?" Fiona could hardly believe his words.

"No. It wasn't quite like that. I've seen those films, mademoiselle. This was more like she'd wrapped it around her lower face for protection from germs or something. It looked to be made of silk and she coughed a few times. She whispered that she'd been ill and that she needed to come to this car for coffee as she couldn't find her steward and her throat was sore and needed to be warmed. I poured her a cup and she left."

"What color was her hair?"

"Well, that's another thing—"

"Oh for the love of Pete, forget it. Just forget it." Fiona twirled around and stalked back to her compartment. She went inside and shut the door hard to make it clear to the steward that she was not happy with him at all. She realized she was panting in anger.

Once she regained control over her breathing, she sat on the bed and opened the letter. Her stomach clenched as she read the words again. This time slowly and deliberately.

*Miss Vancleave:*

*Your secret is known. You won't get away with it. Remember what happened to Mata Hari. If you don't want to suffer the same fate, give up your game now. Spies get executed.*

*From: a patriot*

Fiona shuddered at the threat in the letter. She had no

idea why someone would think she was a spy, but that didn't mean whomever had written the letter wasn't deadly serious about causing her harm. Already there had been a murder onboard and she sure wasn't forgetting about what happened to Cordelia. That could very well have resulted in a second murder.

Determined to get assistance, she attended to her morning routine as quickly as humanly possible and then put on a cream shirtwaist dress with navy blue trim. She combed her hair and placed her hat at a rakish angle to give herself some confidence. She left her compartment and, ignoring the steward in the corridor, headed to the dining car, hoping Win was there having an early breakfast.

She walked into the dining area and scanned the room. No Win as yet, but Lady Sarah Marchman was seated by herself at one of the tables at the far side near the front of the car. Not wanting to sit alone in case someone undesirable tried to insinuate themselves at her table, Fiona approached Lady Sarah.

Before she arrived at the other woman's table, Lady Sarah waved Fiona over. "Come and join me, dear."

"I'd love to." Fiona pulled out the chair across from her friend. "How are you this morning? You're up early."

"That husband of mine is rattling around our compartment trying to be quiet but that's when he always makes the most noise. He was practicing his lecture and attempting not to wake me but it didn't work." Lady Sarah laughed. "I decided it would be better for me to get up and get out of there before our marriage ended."

"I'm glad you decided to come. I was up early, too, and am happy not to have to eat alone."

The waiter arrived and took their orders.

"How was your evening? Did you get your work done that you wanted to finish before we get to Istanbul?"

"I *did* and I want to apologize for dashing out of the lounge last night. I feel much more prepared today for the presentation I have to make."

Fiona didn't tell Lady Sarah that some of her notes seemed to be missing and she'd searched all through her compartment. She decided she must have accidently left those research papers at her flat in Worchester. It was regrettable that she'd left them but luckily, she had a good memory and was sure she'd be able to tough it out without those notes.

"I'm glad. You seem more relaxed today. I confess I was a little startled at how intense you were about not having that drink."

Fiona grimaced. "I get a little snappy sometimes. It makes my mother despair of me."

"I bet your mum was a strict taskmaster when you were a child."

"What makes you say that?"

"You seem extremely well put together for someone of your young age. One must believe that your parents had something to do with that."

Fiona fiddled with her silverware, flipping her butter knife onto its edge. "I'm not sure. My mother has always been an angel. She's gentle and sweet but my father is the complete opposite. He's a bit of an authoritarian and dictates what happens in the home. I rarely stood up to him when I was living there. He ran the household almost like a branch of the military."

"Really? He was as bad as all that?"

"Oh yes. He was awful. I was glad when I got my job and was able to move out. Even though the little flat I live in with my roommate is tiny, I have a freedom there that I've never experienced before." Fiona peeked up from the knife to make eye contact with Lady Sarah. "I'm sure you can't relate to such a father what with yours being a member of the peerage. I imagine a duke as a father is kind of tough, too."

The waiter arrived with Fiona's plate of eggs and kippers. He sat it on the table then placed Lady Sarah's boiled egg in its silver cup on a white china plate in front of her. He handed Lady Sarah a silver egg cutter and a spoon. "Milady, I noted that you've used your spoon for your coffee so I brought you an extra."

As the waiter backed away, Lady Sarah smiled and thanked him. She turned back to Fiona. "My father isn't so bad but it sounds almost like yours is a fascist and runs his household in that manner."

Fiona resisted the urge to slap her hand over her mouth but just barely. She'd gone and stepped in it now.

Dear God, how was she going to explain that? She sucked in a breath and shook her head. "Sorry I made it sound like that. He's really not that bad. You know how we young women sometimes exaggerate."

"I somehow think you're one of those that wouldn't embellish, my dear."

"You'd be wrong. Remember, I'm a librarian. I've had my head stuck in books so long that I may imagine things that aren't there. After all, isn't fiction always more fun than reality?" Fiona tried to laugh off her faux pas but it seemed as if Lady Sarah could see right through her act.

Lady Sarah cut her egg open with the utensil and added some salt to the top. "I disagree. I think a librarian would be sensible and serious since you have to assist people in all kinds of boring research, don't you?"

"We do—"

A loud noise startled her and Fiona stopped midsentence. She focused on the commotion at the door. Abigail Perry stood right inside and screeched as soon as Fiona made eye contact with her. Abigail had a wild look about her. Her hair was mussed and her makeup had run down her face. Mascara pooled at the bottom of her eyes making her appear deranged.

Fiona gaped at the woman then glanced over at Lady Sarah. "What do you think is going on with Mrs. Perry?"

"I'm sure I don't know, dear, but watch out. Here she comes."

Chairs crashed and fell against each other as Abigail made her way across the room. The waiters all stood to the side and watched, none daring to interfere. Fiona hoped the woman was coming over to Lady Sarah since she seemed distraught and they had appeared to be friends last night.

Abigail came to a stop in front of Fiona. She flung the closest chair out of the way. It sailed across the space between the tables. Fiona looked at it as it landed near the next one over. As she glanced back up at the woman now standing beside her, Abigail leaned over and smacked Fiona across the face.

Shocked, Fiona recoiled, shoved her own chair back, and tried to rise.

Abigail whacked her in the face again, this time with the back of her hand. Her wedding ring hit Fiona's cheek.

Fiona reached up to her face and blood seeped though her fingers. Appalled, she gasped, "Why are you hitting me?"

"Now see here. Stop that right now."

The chief conductor strode across the room but before he could get to their table, Abigail punched Fiona again. This time with her balled-up fist.

Fiona cried out in pain.

The conductor pulled Abigail away. As he carried her out of the dining car, she yelled, "You're going to be arrested and I hope you die in jail." The crazed woman kicked at the conductor as he took her out.

As soon as they were gone, one of the waiters dashed over with a linen napkin and a bowl of water. Pushing aside Fiona's breakfast plate, he set the bowl on the table. "This is warm water, Miss Vancleave. Let me see about cleaning that wound."

Fiona stood. "I think not. You all stood by as that woman attacked me. I think I'll tend to my own wounds in my compartment. You can have my steward drop me off a medical kit with some gauze and creams but I'll see to myself." With as much dignity as she could muster, Fiona strode out of the room.

Once she was out of the dining car and no one else was around, she leaned against the wall and tried to gain control of her racing heart. She clutched her chest as if that would help calm her down.

Dear God what the heck had just happened? Why did that woman lose her mind like that? *What did she mean by having me arrested?*

Deciding to worry later about Abigail Perry and her crazy words, Fiona pushed away from the wall and hurried down the corridor to her compartment.

Inside, she stood in front of the mirror and assessed the damage.

Stepping close to the glass, she inspected the cut. It was over her cheekbone and kind of deep. It still oozed blood.

A knock on the door pulled her from her inspection. "Yes? Who's there?"

"It's the steward, miss. I have a first aid kit for you."

"Come in. It's not locked."

The steward entered and when he saw Fiona's face, he blanched. "Let me help you. You're going to need stitches. I was a medic in the Great War. Can I fix that for you?"

"I don't want a scar. Can you fix it so I don't? I don't know why she did this. Why would she attack me for no reason? I don't know what to do."

Fiona knew she was getting hysterical but she couldn't help it. She won this trip of a lifetime and now she was going to be scarred for that lifetime. It didn't make any sense.

She burst into tears and threw herself down on the seat. She hid her face in her hands and sobbed.

The steward sat beside her. "Come on, mademoiselle. Let me see the cut. It needs attention."

She faced him and uncovered her eyes. "It's awful."

He took her by the chin and turned her face to the side so he could inspect the damage. "I think I can fix you up and there will be minimal scarring. Will you let me try?"

She nodded and he got to work.

⁊⊃⁊⊃

When Win and Cordelia arrived at the dining car, Mack stood outside the door. Win greeted him. "How are you this morning? I didn't take you for too much money last night, did I?"

"Did you hear what happened?"

"No. What?" Win's stomach lurched. What else could possibly have happened in the few hours since he'd gone to bed?

"Donald Perry was found dead this morning in the baggage area."

"*What*? How?" Shocked, Win could hardly believe that yet another person had died on this trip.

"He was stabbed."

"Oh no." Cordelia swooned. "It's too much. Not another stabbing."

Mack caught her. "It gets worse, I'm afraid."

Win paced in front of the door to the dining car and stepped aside as a couple of passengers entered. "What can be worse than another dead man?"

"He was found with some of Fiona Vancleave's papers in his hands. Covered with blood, I might add."

"Fiona?" asked Cordelia.

"Yes, your friend, Fiona. Not only that, the widow Perry found Miss Vancleave at breakfast with Lady Sarah and attacked her."

"Attacked Lady Sarah or Fiona?" Win asked.

"Fiona. She was last seen returning to her compartment with blood streaming down her face."

Win's heart dropped to his knees. "She was hurt?"

"That's what I hear. I was going that way to check

on her when I saw you arrive. I thought you might want to come with me."

"Of course we're coming." Cordelia stepped past Mack and strode down the corridor. "Come on. I need to be sure she's all right."

Win smiled at Mack. "No one tells Cordelia no. Better get moving." He forced himself to walk at a regular pace, even though all he wanted to do was run as quickly as he could to make sure that Fiona was fine.

They arrived at Fiona's door as the steward was coming out. He had a bowl filled with bloody rags. Win almost lost his composure at the sight. He was saved from making a fool of himself by Cordelia's squeal.

"Is that Fiona's blood?" she asked the steward.

"It is, but it looks worse than it really is. She's going to be fine. A bit of stitches was all that she needed. I was a medic and I set her to rights. She's going to have a black eye and a swollen cheek for a while but she's a real strong lady. She's going to recover." The steward walked toward the serving area near the end of the corridor. "Excuse me while I attend to my other duties."

Cordelia banged on Fiona's door. "Fi. Open up, dearest. It's me and Win. We want to see you. Open the door, darling."

Win stood beside Mack and tried to hold himself together.

He didn't know why he was terrified to see her. He wanted her to be all right but he was also wondering why the dead man was holding her papers. What kind of trouble might she be in?

The door opened a slight bit. Cordelia barged into the chamber and let out a gasp.

Win and Mack followed her in. Cordelia pulled Fiona into a hug and held on to her.

"Oh honey. I'm so sorry. What happened? Why did that woman think you had anything to do with her husband's murder?"

Fiona stepped back and stared at Cordelia with her mouth open. When she appeared to recover herself, she asked, "Murder? What murder?"

Win winced at the damage to Fiona's face. He opened his mouth to say something but Mack spoke first. "It seems Mr. Perry was stabbed to death."

Fiona gasped. "*Really*? When?"

"Either late last night or early this morning," Mack said.

"Why did she think I was part of it? I had to be the first person to leave the lounge last night and came here to work on my notes. I didn't leave my quarters until I woke around six and went to breakfast. I don't remember if her husband was in the bar but I know I didn't even *see* him, much less kill him."

Cordelia took Fiona by the arm and pulled her over to sit on the bench seat. "I'm sorry to tell you that Mack heard that Mr. Perry was found with some of your notes in his hand. They were bloody."

Fiona gasped. "No." She shook her head. "There's no way he had my documents."

Mack knelt in front of her. "I'm sorry to say it, too, but I've spoken to the conductor and he confirms it. I'm surprised that they haven't come by to talk to you about it."

"Have you noticed anything missing from your compartment?" Win asked. He could barely stand to look at her. She was so pale and the marks of the crazed Perry woman's hands on Fiona's face were apparent. There were the black stitches and a red welt as well as what appeared to be a palm print.

She nodded. "I did find last night that some of my notes on the layout of the train and the various stations it has stopped at over the years were missing. I figured I accidently left them at home. I never dreamed someone had been in here stealing my things."

"That doesn't sound good, Fi. I'm afraid they're going to suspect you." Cordelia patted Fiona's arm. "We know you didn't do it but the police may think you did since the dead man had your papers."

Fiona looked over Mack's head at Win where he leaned on the window. "What am I going to do?"

Win stared at her for a few moments before answering. Thoughts raced through his mind as he recalled the conversation in the corridor where Perry accused Fiona of being a Nazi spy. To be honest with himself, he wanted it not to be true; but it seemed a bit odd that she'd been accused and the very next morning, the man who said those things was dead. With her papers in hand.

It was definitely suspicious.

He must have taken too long to respond as tears came to Fiona's eyes and she said, "You think I did it, don't you?"

"Surely not. Anyone can see that you're too small to have overpowered that huge man," Cordelia said.

Mack rose and took the seat next to her. He held on to her hand. "Come on, Fiona. You know there are going to be some hard questions to answer. Let's go over a few now that I'm sure the police will be asking, all right?"

"I know we need to do that, Mack but I want to hear what Win has to say first." Fiona stared at up at Win. "Don't you have anything to say at all?"

The muscle of his cheek twitched. "I think Mack is right. We need to get you prepared for questioning."

"You *do* think I did it, don't you?" the tears flowed unheeded down Fiona's face.

What could he say? He wasn't sure. He'd seen female assassins before and it wasn't outside the realm of possibility that Fiona was a cunning spy. He hated that he'd been trained to doubt everyone when she so needed to be comforted; but he couldn't bring himself to give her platitudes when he had his doubts.

Cordelia stomped her foot. "Winchester Barrington the fourth, you should be ashamed of yourself for thinking my dear Fi could stab a man to death like that. You need to apologize to her right now."

"Cordelia, you can't force the man to believe me. Let it go." Fiona shook her head and turned her back on Win. "Help me, Mack. Please."

The tone of her voice in her plea to Mack wrenched Win's gut. She sounded so bereft and alone. He wanted so much to believe in her but didn't know how to get there.

Mack didn't let go of Fiona's hand. "Of course I'll help you, Fiona. Let's start at the beginning, shall we? When did you get back to your compartment and find the papers missing? What time was it, do you know?"

"I had a drink with Monsieur Cassel in the lounge, then on my way out, I was stopped by Lady Sarah Marchman and Abigail Perry—" Fiona gasped. "Wait. Do you think they waylaid me in order to give Mr. Perry a chance to come to my compartment and steal my notes?"

"I hardly think they would do that, dear. What was in your notes that would be important to a wool merchant?" Cordelia asked.

"Wait a second. Let's think about that a minute," Win offered, a twinge of hope rising in his chest. "Maybe Mrs. Perry wanted to kill her own husband and set you up as the culprit."

It made more sense than the whole Fiona/spy thing.

"Why would she want to do that?" Cordelia asked.

"More importantly, why would she send her husband to get Fiona's papers? What would she tell him was in them to make him want to steal them?" Mack asked.

"We both saw Perry last night, Mack, and you know he accused Fiona of being a Nazi spy. Maybe the wife told him she'd seen some evidence?" Win wasn't sure he should be divulging the man's comment about Fiona being a spy but he did want to help her out of this mess. Spy or no spy.

"Wait. *What*? He said what?" Fiona wailed.

"He said you were a Nazi spy." Mack patted her hand. "Nonsense of course."

Fiona reached into the pocket of her dress. She pulled out an envelope. "I quite forgot about this in all the excitement of being punched and having the stitches. I got this outside my door this morning and I took it down to the dining car hoping to find you—" She looked up at Win and held out the letter. "—to ask you what I should do about it. You weren't there and I sat down with Lady Sarah to eat and wait for you to show up. Before you got there, Abigail Perry attacked me and I came back here."

"Let me see that." Win took it from her hand and slid a piece of paper out of the envelope. He opened it and read in silence. When he was done, he silently handed it over to Mack.

Mack read it and before he could say anything, Cordelia snatched it from him. "Let me see it, too." She glanced over at Fiona. "Men, humpf."

Once Cordelia finished, she gaped at Fiona. "Oh dear, this is scary, Fi. Very scary. You needed to report this right away to the conductor."

"I wanted to get Win's help first but now I see that I shouldn't have held on to it. It makes me really look guilty and if I'd given it over before we knew Mr. Perry was dead, it would seem less damaging."

Win shook his head. "I'm not sure that it matters in what order it comes to the attention of the authorities, Fiona. It doesn't look good no matter what. It gives you motive for sure."

"If I'd turned it in earlier, it wouldn't appear that I had a motive since I wouldn't be keeping a secret. Now it's like I was keeping it quiet and killed him to prevent him from talking." Fiona pulled her hand from Mack's, flung herself on the bench, and sobbed into her arms.

Cordelia patted Fiona on the head. "Buck up, old girl. We need to stay clear-headed. Do you have any clue where it came from or who wrote it?"

Fiona sat up. "I have no idea. All I know is that this was outside my door. I have no idea who wrote it or why they would suspect me of being a spy."

"You *do* know you have to tell the authorities about this. You can't keep it a secret." Cordelia handed the note back to Mack. "Don't you agree, Mr. Plant?"

"Speaking as a police officer, yes."

"I know. Like I said, I wanted to have Win help me with it earlier but got side-tracked when that woman hit me." Fiona wiped the tears from her face and stood. "I guess there's nothing else to do except see if I can find the head conductor and see if he'll lead me to whomever is in charge of the investigation into Mr. Perry's death."

"I'll go with you." Win held his arm out to her but before she could slide her hand inside the crook of his elbow, there was a hard knock at the door and a voice said, "Open up, Miss Vancleave."

# Chapter 12

Where observation is concerned, chance favours only the prepared mind. ~ *Louis Pasteur, French Chemist, 1822-1895*

Win opened the compartment door to find three men standing in the corridor. The burliest one spoke, "Please step back, sir. We're here to speak to Mademoiselle Vancleave."

Fiona stepped forward. "I'm Miss Vancleave."

"We're the police. We boarded at Bucharest and need to question you about the death of Mr. Donald Perry. His wife has given a statement that implicates you. We need to ask you about this matter."

"Wait a moment here. She's implicated? Have you

even looked into the possibility that she was set up? Aren't wives usually the first suspect?" Win could scarcely believe it. On the word of the deceased's wife, they were going to make her their suspect? He was sure they knew about the fact that Fiona's papers were found with the deceased's body. That alone wasn't enough to actually accuse her of murder until they'd at least questioned her and anyone else who had access to her compartment, and before they got any fingerprints off the knife.

He could see them jumping to conclusions if they knew about the letter accusing Fiona of being a Nazi as well as all the rest of the evidence. Right now all they had was some papers and the word of the wife. This was bad. He wasn't sure she'd be able to get out of this snare she found herself in. He was at a loss as to how to help her.

"Yes, sir, she is our main suspect. Now, you'll excuse us." The burly man took hold of Fiona's upper arm. "Come with us to the library area. That's where we're doing the questioning."

"May I accompany Miss Vancleave?" Win asked.

"No, I'm afraid not." The man led Fiona out the door. "Please excuse us."

Fiona looked back at them over her shoulder as they took her away. She seemed so lost and forlorn, Win's heart sank and his gut burned.

"Maybe we need to get to work to figure out who really did this," Mack said.

Cordelia tugged at Mack's arm. "No maybe about it, Mr. Plant. We *have* to help her. She's a little librarian who'd never hurt anyone. No way she did this awful thing. You're a big, bad city policeman and you have the skill to solve this. With your experience and my brother's brains, you have all you need to get her out of trouble. Let's go back to our compartment and put our heads to this."

Win turned toward the other end of the corridor. "You two go on down there, Cordelia. I'll join you in a few minutes."

"Where are you going?" Cordelia called after him.

"I'm going to talk to the steward to see if he knows where that note that Fiona got this morning came from."

"Good idea. We'll meet you at the compartment," Cordelia said.

Determined to find out what really happened and who left the note, Win approached the steward and questioned him. After learning the same thing the man had earlier told Fiona—that there was both a man and a woman in the corridor around six am—Win decided to stroll to the back of the train to the same area his sister described when she re-boarded the train.

He strolled around that section of the train, looking in a few boxes and a couple of bags that were scattered about. Nothing really stood out to him but there were some recognizable mint candy wrappers on the floor. Win knelt down and pocketed a couple of them. It seemed a bit odd that the Cassel man would be littering them all over the train. What kind of person did that? Yes, this was the very back end of the train but it still didn't make sense to use it as a rubbish bin.

In that moment, Win decided that either the man was a sloppy jerk or that someone was setting him up to take the fall for all the things happening on the journey. He didn't really believe the man was stupid enough to leave the distinctive candy coverings in his wake, if he was a criminal.

Once he was satisfied he'd covered the area, Win walked to the baggage compartment to check it out. He convinced one of the conductors to unlock the area by telling him that he needed something from his own trunk stored there. The man let him in and showed him where the trunk was stored. The steward left him with instructions to come find him once he was done so he could lock the compartment.

Win could hardly believe his luck. The steward actually left him alone to look around. He had no idea what he was trying to find but his gut told him there was something to be found in this part of the train. He knew he was going to be able to get closer to solving the murders now.

He plundered around for a while and was about to give up and call it a bust, when he happened upon a large hatbox sitting on top of a black trunk with a lot of stickers from various European hotels on it.

The trunk sat at an odd angle and some white fabric

spilled out of one side of it as if it were hastily throw inside and shut in a hurry.

"What have we here?" Win asked himself as he flipped the lid off and tugged out the fabric. It was a long fur trimmed coat. The steward had described this coat to a T. The woman in the corridor outside Fiona's room wore such a coat. He took a deep breath. *Could this be it?*

Win inspected the coat with care. On the lookout for anything distinctive, he searched the outside as well as the pockets.

He felt along the front and back as well as in the lining. In the left pocket, he found a hankie. He opened it to see if there were any initials but there weren't. It *did* have a distinctive trim around the edge but it would be quite a job figuring out if there was any woman on board who had others to match. He wondered if Cordelia would recognize it as belonging to one of the other ladies on board.

He also noticed that one of the creamy white horn buttons on the front of the garment was missing. The third one down on the placket of the coat. There was also a smaller one missing on the cuff of the left sleeve.

Win reached into the other pocket and found a small pouch of pipe tobacco. "Hmm. A woman who smokes a pipe? Or was she holding the packet for her husband or lover?" He placed it in his own pocket along with the handkerchief, put the coat back in the trunk, as best he could to match how it was when he found it, and left the room to find the steward and make his way back to his own compartment.

He wished he had found the black scarf that the man who saw the mysterious woman had described but he was satisfied with what he did uncover. At least it was something that might help Fiona.

 espes

After several hours of questioning, they allowed Fiona to return to her compartment. The police had warned her that she could not leave the train when it arrived at Istanbul other than to accompany them to the local station. Since the police presumed that the crime took place in Bucharest, she was expected to return there to face charges if the investigation concluded that she was the culprit.

She almost vomited when they said that. Even though she knew she was innocent, she was terrified that they would blame her anyway. It would be easy for them to do since there was that unexplained letter calling her a Mata Hari and all the unrest on the continent that already existed. She'd given them the letter only because she knew if she didn't, whoever sent it to her might pass on the information to the authorities. If she hadn't turned it over, it would look worse for her.

She knew if they did a cursory investigation into her family, they'd find out about her father's fascist tendencies. Never mind that she'd moved out due to his politics, it would be assumed that she believed the same as he did. She never would have believed such a thing could be happening to her.

In her cabin, she tugged off her perky little hat from the morning that looked as wilted and sad as she felt now. She still could scarcely take in the situation in which she found herself. A murder suspect of all things. Last week she was at work amongst all the books she loved and now, here she was all the way almost to the easternmost edge of the continent basically all alone and at the mercy of foreign police.

So much for being excited about winning a contest for a trip to Istanbul.

Fiona tossed the small hat at the rack above the seat, fully expecting it to fall to the floor but it landed right on top, settling in with a little jostle as it hit the shelf. She giggled a little hysterically and to stop herself from collapsing in tears again, she sat and picked up her notepad and a pen.

She needed to write to her mother to let her know what was happening in case she was never allowed to return home.

That thought made her lips quiver, but determined to soldier on, she opened the pad and started to write. Before she'd finished the salutation on the note, there was a quick succession of three raps on the door followed by, "Fiona. Open up, it's Cordelia."

Letting out a deep sigh and bracing herself for the tornado that was Cordelia, Fiona set her pad and pen down and stepped over to the door.

"Come in. I'm glad for the company since I've been confined to quarters by the police. It looks like I'm stuck here for the duration, unless someone comes forward and confesses, which we both know won't happen."

Cordelia flounced in and flopped down on the far end of bench seat from Fiona. She stretched her legs out and crossed them at the ankle.

"I heard they said you had to stay here. They didn't say you couldn't have visitors though so I came down. I also asked Barry what he could do about getting you cut loose but he said he had no pull to do that."

"Why would he have any influence at all?"

"I just thought he could use his powers of persuasion to let the authorities know there is no way that you're a spy, much less a killer."

"I don't think that they would believe a man from the United States on that—and besides, I think Win thinks I did it." Fiona was surprised at how much merely saying the words hurt her to the soul. When had she developed such a thin skin? She mulled that over for a second and realized it wasn't a change in her sensitivity, rather, it was that man in particular who she wanted to have a good opinion of her. She was so wrapped in her thoughts that she missed what Cordelia was saying.

"Did you hear me?" Cordelia peered into Fiona's

face. "Are you still in there? Did the police rob you of your senses?"

"Of course not. I was thinking."

"About how you can get away?"

"Huh?" Fiona shook her head, unsure she'd heard her friend correctly. "What?"

"I *said* that I spoke to Mack when Barry said he wouldn't help you escape. Mack thinks we can pull it off."

Fiona could scarcely believe her ears. This woman was crazy. What was she thinking? "Are you *insane*? You actually asked your brother to help me escape? Why would he? And for that matter, why would *I*? Do you think I want to live my life as some kind of fugitive? No way. I've been *falsely* accused. If I run, I'll be convicted for that alone."

"You don't have to get so huffy. I'm only trying to help."

"I know you have good intentions, but running away is *not* the answer."

"But you have no idea what kind of prisons they have in Bucharest."

"Neither do you. It could be a nice one." Fiona tried to laugh but a sob escaped instead.

Cordelia slid over and hugged Fiona. "We'll think of something."

"I hope so. We're running out of time. The train will be in Istanbul tomorrow."

"I know. I'll be back later this evening with Mack. We're going to put our heads together and see what we can do to help figure out who the murderer is. Do you want me to bring you anything special to eat?"

"I presume the steward will bring me some dinner." Fiona made a face. "This all started with that sweet Lucien getting killed. I wish we knew why someone wanted to kill him because it *has* to be related. That could be the key to figuring this whole thing out."

"I'll ask Mack what he knows about that. I saw him talking to the authorities, right after Lucien died. Maybe he has some information he hasn't shared."

"You sure have gotten chummy with Mr. Plant. What have you told him about your 'marriage'?"

Cordelia blushed. "Nothing, really, although I want to tell him that Barry is my brother. I know Barry would kill me, though." She gasped. "Not literally, of course."

Fiona laughed. "I think I knew that."

"I hope so. My brother has a temper but he's pretty good at controlling it." She paused and then added, "Most of the time, anyway."

"That's good to know. I have no siblings but I have a father with anger problems and it's not fun to live like that. I'm glad you and Win get along so well."

"Speaking of getting along with my brother, I noticed he seems to be turning on the charm with you. Are you interested in him?"

"Of course not."

"Why not? He's handsome, educated, well-spoken, and can afford a wife. What's not to like?" Cordelia winked.

"That's all true."

"Then why aren't you interested in him?"

"He's out of my league."

"What does that even mean, Fi?"

"It means I'm a lowly librarian and he's a wealthy business owner in the upper class. I'm a barely middle class person. In the grand scheme of things, we should've never even met."

"Ahh, but you did. How do we know you winning the contest wasn't divine intervention so you could meet and marry my brother?"

Fiona laughed so hard that tears came. She wiped them with the heels of her hands and once she caught her breath, she replied, "Now I know you've lost your mind."

"My brother and I are *not* snobs, Fi, and I'm hurt that you think we'd be of the opinion you're not good enough for our family. It almost sounds like *you* think you're too good—you and your middle class values."

"Oh, Cordelia, I'm so sorry. I didn't mean to offend you."

"You know, my family has been falsely accused of snobbery before by a boy I met and thought I was in love with. He ended up breaking off our relationship because he thought my parents looked down on him." Cordelia wiped the corner of her eye. "It broke my heart. I thought he was going to propose and he broke up with me instead. Don't let your financial position make you push my brother away."

"Why are you saying all this? Has he said anything to you?" Fiona couldn't believe the way the conversation had turned. She'd gone from worrying about murder charges and jail in a foreign country to discussing the ins and outs of romance with a Barrington.

"No. He hasn't said a word to me but I know him. The way he looks at you reminds me of the way he looks at his yellow 1937 Rolls-Royce Phantom III."

"He looks at me like a car?"

"No, you ninny." Cordelia swatted Fiona's hand. "He loves that car more than anything he's ever loved—besides me and our parents, that is—and when he eyes you, he has the same besotted facial expression as when he stares at that car."

Fiona giggled. "I know I feel better knowing that I may rate up there with a hunk of metal."

"You should." Cordelia nodded sagely. "It's a gorgeous piece of metal. At least in Barry's eyes it is."

Fiona shook her head then picked up her note pad. "Do you mind if I finish writing a letter to my mum about what's happened? I need to tell her about all this."

Cordelia nodded at the pad of paper. "Not at all. Go ahead."

"Will you make sure it's mailed if I'm taken to the police station as soon as we arrive in Istanbul?" Determined not to cry again, Fiona stared down at the sheet until the tears pooled in her eyes dried and she had some semblance of control. Once she knew she wasn't going to sob, she glanced up at Cordelia for an answer. "Will you?"

Cordelia embraced her. "Of course, darling. Of course, I will but I hope it won't be necessary."

"Me, too." Fiona wiped her face and started writing.

# Chapter 13

Every form of addiction is bad, no matter whether the narcotic be alcohol or morphine or idealism. ~ *Carl Gustav Jung, Swiss Psychologist, 1875-1961*

The meeting between the five men broke up an hour before dinner was served in the dining car. Win and Plant stepped into the corridor outside the library where they'd gathered. Behind them came the head conductor and the two Turkish men who Win had noticed the first day of the trip. He was pleased to have learned in the meeting that they were actually undercover Istanbul policemen.

They were on the train on a tip that drug smugglers

were on board with a cache of heroin that they were transporting across Europe to sell in Turkey.

Win turned to the elder of the Turkish men, Ahmet. "I'll lead you to the area of the train where Cordelia saw the group gathered around the small packages before she was tossed off. I think that's going to be your best chance to catch the men or women behind the drugs. It makes sense to me that they would try to get rid of Cordelia since she discovered their lair."

The younger of the men, Faruk, said, "I agree. I think we're going to need to have a discussion with your sister. She could very well hold the answers to our case. I'm glad you told us what she saw."

Mack clapped Win on the shoulder. "I was more relieved to find out Cordelia's not your wife than to learn what she saw at the back of the train. I still can't believe you brought her with you on your mission. I guess what I really can't fathom is that the War Department let you do it."

"I needed a spouse in a hurry and you need to stop talking about it out here in the open. I only shared that information in an attempt to try to get to the bottom of whatever is going on here. I still plan to continue the act until we debark." Win cringed as he glanced around to be sure that only the people who'd been in on the meeting were in the area.

He hated that he had to blow his cover. He'd needed to be honest with the conductor and the police if he hoped to help Fiona out of her troubles as well as figure out his own mystery.

As for Cordelia, and Mack's palpable relief that she was single, he'd leave that issue up to his sister. She was a pro at handling men's attentions, wanted or not. Win had a feeling that Mack's attentions would be welcomed. It wouldn't be bad if she ended up with the man from Chicago. He seemed like an upstanding chap and one who could handle the boisterous Cordelia. God help him if he chose that path but Win really wouldn't mind having the guy as a brother-in-law.

"Once we look over the back of the train, I'll take you to talk to Cordelia." Win headed down the corridor with the others following behind.

After they'd inspected the room where Cordelia was attacked and tossed off the train, Win led them all to the baggage compartment where he'd found the coat. He wasn't sure if the murders were related to the heroin smuggling or not but he wanted to share what information he had since the Turks had shared with him.

When they were all ready to leave the baggage area, Win turned to Plant. "Will you take them back to my compartment to interview Cordelia about her ordeal while I go and check on Fiona?"

"I'll be glad to do so but what about the lovely Miss Vancleave? Does she know your secret?"

Win shook his head in confusion. "What secret?" Of course, Fiona didn't know his real purpose on the train.

"That you're actually a single man." Mack grinned. "Dare I say that I think the girl has a crush on you?"

"I'm not so sure about the crush thing, but yes, Fiona *does* know Cordelia is my sister and not my wife. I told her when Cordelia went missing. I was distraught and it came out. She's been good enough to keep it quiet."

"I like that little librarian. She has good sense. A man wouldn't go wrong in pursuing her."

"I think you need to hurry on to Cordelia."

Win wanted nothing more than for the blasted man to be gone. He wasn't entirely sure of his feelings for Fiona, since in the back of his mind he wasn't positive exactly what and who she was. He sure didn't want to talk to Mack Plant about all the thoughts and worries swirling in his head.

"Sure. We're off. I'll make sure they treat her properly."

"I'm sure they will be kind. She's not a suspect herself. It'll be fine for her to give her statement to them since she's already given it twice before. I'll be along in a few minutes."

Mack winked. "Take your time. Enjoy Miss Vancleave's company. I have this interview under control."

Win stared at Mack in silence then shook his head. The man was entirely too gleeful now that he knew Cordelia was a free woman. Mack grinned, saluted, and walked away, the other three men following in his wake.

છ્જ્જ

A knock at her door startled Fiona. She'd been sitting with her head leaning on the seat back with her eyes closed.

She sat up and ran a hand over her hair before she called out, "Just a moment." She reached for the formerly perky hat that still looked as sad as it did when she first tossed it on the shelf. She set it on her head and poked in the hatpin to hold it in place. No sense in looking like a criminal yet. Might as well put on the trappings of society while she still could.

The knock came again. "Coming." Fiona stood and went to the door. "Who is it?"

"Win. Let me in for a minute, please."

Knowing her mother would disapprove since she had no chaperone, but not caring, Fiona opened the door.

Win stepped inside. His body heat making the room uncomfortably warm, he stood beside her. "Are you all right?"

"I'm doing fair. A bit terrified, but physically I'm still breathing and my heart's still pumping."

He smiled down at her. "Glad to hear it. That you're still alive, that is."

"For now. I imagine if I'm convicted of murder, I'll be executed." Fiona was amazed at how easy the words came out. She didn't even break down when she said it. Could she be getting used to the idea?

"Don't say such things." Win placed his hands on her upper arms and rubbed them up and down. "I can't imagine that you'll be convicted."

"I *can.* I'm in a foreign country with no lawyer, no family, and a dead man with my papers in his hands with blood all over them. There's no need in pretending this is going to be easy for me. I didn't do it but I daresay everyone, including you—don't deny it—thinks I did. You have to admit that the evidence against me is damning."

"Come. Sit down. I want to talk to you about all that." Win led her over to the bench seat and they both sat.

"Talk about what? Cordelia was already here telling me that she asked you to help me escape from the train. You have to know I can't live on the run. No way can I do anything less than honorable. I have to face the charges and hope for an acquittal since I didn't do it. If I'm convicted, I'll face that when the time comes."

"I want to help you, Fiona, but not to escape. That was a crazy idea Cordelia had. I asked her if she'd spoken to you about it, because I didn't think there was any way you had agreed to such a plan."

"I didn't. She thought that up all by herself and I had no idea."

"I *do* need to ask some tough questions, though. Can you allow me to ask some things without getting offended?"

Fiona drew back and stared at him for a moment. "It depends on what they are."

"Fair enough." Win nodded. "If I ask something that makes you uncomfortable, let me know and I'll either explain why I think we need it or I'll rephrase it, does that sound all right?"

"Yes. Go ahead. Ask away."

"Are you a Nazi spy?"

"Wow." Fiona recoiled. "That's a loaded question to start off with." She could sense her blood pressure rise but controlled her anger. This was most certainly one of the first questions that any prosecutor would ask and had, in fact, been asked by the policemen already. It wouldn't do any good to get mad at Win over it when he was trying to help her.

"Will you answer it? Not that if you really *are* a spy I would expect you to admit to it without being tortured."

"Then why ask? The police did, too. Why would either of you ask if you know the answer will be no?"

Win smiled. "There's a lot we as investigators and trained interrogators can learn about a person from the way they react to a question."

"You're a trained *interrogator*? I thought you were an engineer or something like that."

"I am. Actually, I'm both. I work for my family business but I also work for the War Department when they need my expertise. Remember, I told you that when Cordelia went missing?"

"I know you did but why would the War Department need you? You work as an engineer. How does that translate to interrogation? I'm confused."

Fiona's heart sank. Was he really here to help her or was he interested in convicting her of espionage and murder? Why would he tell her he was with the War Department if he wasn't? This was the second time he'd mentioned that.

"I'm not really supposed to tell you this but I'm on the train for other reasons than I told you earlier. Now that there's been this second murder and it appears that you're being framed for it, I think I need to let you in on the secret."

"What's that, Win? And why would I trust that you believe that I've been set up? Just a little while ago, you thought I was a criminal—no, don't look at me like that—you know you *did* think I'm guilty. And for all I know, you still do."

"You're right. I admit it. I had a few moments of concern but once I left and got a chance to explore the train, I changed my mind. I don't think you did anything wrong at all."

"Why? What changed your mind?"

Fiona stood and paced around the small space. Sitting beside Win was making her uncomfortable. He seemed to suck up all the oxygen in the room. She was hot and the sweat dripped down her spine. His closeness was too much for her.

He smelled of pipe tobacco, shaving cream, and some kind of spicy cologne. The combination was hard to resist.

"I found a white coat in the baggage area and I think that Mr. Perry was killed by the woman who wore it."

She stopped mid-pace. "How do you know it was the wearer who was the murderer and, more importantly, how do you know *I* wasn't the one in it?"

"As you know, the steward saw a woman and a man in the corridor outside this compartment at different times a few minutes before you came out and found the note."

"And what about it?"

"The steward knew you weren't the woman he saw. The coat I found was the one he saw and therefore, we know it wasn't you who left the note for yourself."

Fiona sat on the opposite bench. Staying away from Win was essential to her ability to think. She couldn't sit down beside him again. "How do we figure out who wore the coat?"

"I also found a few things with the coat and want to show them to you to see if you recognize them. Can I do that?"

"Sure. Go ahead, although I don't think it's going to do any good."

"Come sit by me." Win patted the seat beside him. "I'll put them on the table."

"I can see them fine from here."

"No, you need to come closer."

Fiona sighed. She'd have to try to hold it together. She wished Cordelia hadn't planted the idea in her head that this man and she had a future.

If she hadn't, Fiona wouldn't be so nervous.

"Are you coming over here or not? I'm not kidding around, Fiona. You're going to need to be close to these items. I need you to give them a good inspection."

"All right. All right. I'm coming." She stomped over not very gracefully.

Win laughed. "What's wrong with you? You're acting like I'm going to execute you or something."

His words stopped her in her tracks. Execute was the word that scared her the most.

Win leapt to his feet. He approached and reached out for her. "I'm so sorry, Fiona. I didn't mean to say that. I didn't mean anything by it. I really *am* trying to help you and didn't intend to upset you.

She took a step back before he could take hold of her. "It's fine. I can't be so sensitive to the word."

He let his arms drop to his side and retook his seat. "I'm sorry for using it anyway. It was insensitive."

Fiona stepped over and sat. "Let's see what you have."

The first thing Win pulled out was a small bag of tobacco. He handed it to Fiona. "Smell it. Does it smell like any that you've been around on this trip? Anyone you know smoke this kind?"

She took the pouch from him, placed it up to her

nose and took a deep sniff. It was the tobacco she'd smelled on him a few moments before but obviously he hadn't smoked it. She took another deep whiff then shook her head. "It smells kind of familiar but it may be because I smelled it earlier as I sat beside you."

"You could discern that scent in my pocket and in the closed packet? If you did, you have a pretty sensitive nose."

"I guess I do." Fiona shrugged. "I thought it was on your clothes from you smoking it. I *have* seen you with a pipe."

"Half the men on this train smoke pipes so that's not surprising. Think about it for a few moments. Close your eyes and try to picture if you've smelled it anywhere else besides here in your compartment."

Fiona leaned her head on the back of the bench and did as he asked.

After a few moments, she opened her eyes and shook her head. "No. I have nothing."

"All right. Here's the second item." Win pulled out the handkerchief he'd found in the coat and handed it to Fiona. He took the pipe tobacco back and set it on the table.

Turning the handkerchief over in her hand, Fiona smiled. "Now, *this* I recognize."

"It's not yours is it?"

"No." She looked up at him, blinded for a second by tears of relief. "Indeed, it is not mine."

"You know whose it is?"

Fiona wiped away a stray tear that trailed down her cheek. "You bet. This is the break I needed."

Win grinned. "So, put me out of my misery and tell me."

"It's clearly the property of Mrs. Donald Perry." Fiona's smile broadened. "That vixen set me up."

# Chapter 14

*I was more pleased with possessing your heart than with any other happiness. ~ Héloise, French Abbess, 1098-1164*

W ill Abigail Perry deny it's hers?" Win asked. He could scarcely believe that the handkerchief was so recognizable to Fiona, which could very well mean that the murder was solved.

"Of course she will but she won't be able to for long since Lady Marchman also saw it when I did. She'll back me up that it was Mrs. Perry's property. The woman made a big deal about the lace border. It seems they got the lace made in Alençon itself. Special order for their use only." Fiona's voice lifted almost in glee as she uttered the last two words. "What great luck that they were so arrogant to want their own lace pattern as well as for that horrible woman to leave it in her coat pocket."

"We need to think about this for a few minutes before we run off half-cocked and accuse her."

"They didn't hesitate to accuse me and put me here on house arrest in my compartment. Why *shouldn't* we accuse her?"

"We will, believe me, we will. I need a moment to think it over, though." Win held his palm up. "We have a while until we arrive at Istanbul and it may be better to set up a plan to trap her versus a straight out accusation. If she has any cohorts, we want to take them down at the same time."

"I'm going to trust you, Mr. Trained Interrogator, but I have to tell you, I want to walk off this train a free woman when we pull into the station at Istanbul so the clock is running on your plan." Fiona glanced down at her watch and tapped the face. Win leaned over and took hold of her wrist. He pulled the watch toward his eyes.

"What are you doing?"

"Seeing how much time I really have." The act of touching her inflamed his passion and he knew he couldn't resist her for one more moment.

She giggled. "Why?"

He cupped her right cheek with the palm of his hand. Her eyes grew big as he moved his face closer to hers. "Because I want to be sure I have time to do this."

Her breath caught. That small noise in her throat was his undoing. He captured her lips with his and caressed her cheek with the pad of his thumb. Her lips softened and opened slightly to allow his tongue access.

Using his other hand, he cradled her head. His fingers tangled in her hair as he deepened the kiss. Her tongue chased his around her mouth and she let out a small groan of pleasure.

As he continued kissing her, Win's hand slid farther down her cheek and on to the side of her neck. Her pulse raced and he was just egotistical enough to enjoy that it was because of his kiss. He continued to cradle her head and let himself go deeper into the kiss.

After a few more moments of bliss, she pulled back. He let her go and stared at her.

Fiona's breath came fast and heavy and Win enjoyed the view of her chest as it moved up and down in her shirtwaist dress. He knew she had no idea how provocative she looked as her breasts heaved. She truly was an innocent woman.

She finally caught her breath and asked, "What was that all about?"

He grinned. "It was a kiss, Fiona. A very nice kiss, I might add."

Her face flushed and she lowered her eyes. "But why? Why did you do that?"

Win reached under her chin with his index finger. When her gaze met his, he winked. "I've been trying to resist doing that for quite a while now. I finally decided that there was no need for me to try to be a boy scout— although I was one at a time in my life."

She smiled a crooked smile. "Boy scouts do kiss, you know."

"Do they? How do you know that?"

"I had a crush on one when I was in school and he kissed me behind the gymnasium."

"So that's where you learned your skill, huh?" Win ran his hand down her upper arm, "because, I have to tell you Miss Vancleave, that was a pretty spectacular kiss." Fiona ducked her head down once more and he lifted her chin again. "Don't be embarrassed. It was wonderful and I hope you enjoyed it as much as I did."

"I confess it *was* nice. Much nicer than any kiss Billy Watson gave me."

"Billy Watson was the boy scout?"

"Yes." She smiled. "He wasn't very expert. Not like you."

Win poked his lip out in mock horror. "It's not like I kiss every girl I meet, Fiona."

"I'm not so sure of that, Mr. Barrington. You seem like someone who likes to see what effect he can have on a girl."

"You really think so?"

"No." She shook her head. "The more I think about it, the more I remember when I first met you and thought you were so overbearing and scary. I take that statement back. You're more likely to arrest a woman than kiss her."

"And speaking of arresting, as much as I'd like to stay right here and keep kissing you, we need to come up with a plan of action to get the police off you as a suspect and onto Mrs. Perry."

"You don't think the handkerchief is enough?"

"No. It's too easy to explain it away. All she would have to do is say it's hers but she lost it and someone must have picked it up."

"You're right. So what do we do? How can we tie her to the handkerchief, the tobacco, and the coat?"

"I have a suggestion but I'm not sure how you'll feel about it." Win patted Fiona's hand. "It could be dangerous. Very dangerous."

Fiona raised her brows. "More dangerous than being in a prison in a foreign country for a crime I didn't commit?"

"When you put it like that, I guess you're right." He scratched his chin. "Maybe equally dangerous?"

"What's the suggestion?"

"I could take the handkerchief to the dining car and make a big deal about passing it around to see if anyone can identify whom it belongs to, maybe suggesting that it's yours. I can also put the word out that I've been by to talk to you. I can say that I think you're despondent about possibly being charged with murder."

"What good would that do?"

"It could plant the idea in her head that you're suicidal and maybe she will decide to come to your compartment to try to make it look like you'd take your own life either out of guilt or being afraid of jail. It could force her hand."

"And if she comes in my compartment to attack me, you'll catch her in the act?"

Win planted a quick kiss on Fiona's lips. "Exactly."

"I think it's a good plan but how will you carry it out? She'll see you in the corridor if you're out there waiting for her to attack."

"Either Plant or I will be hiding here in the closet. Before she can get to you, we'll catch her."

"I'm game. It's better than sitting here waiting for my fate. Let's get started."

Win stood and pulled Fiona to her feet. He leaned in and pulled her body toward his until they were as close as they could get. He dipped his head and captured her mouth with his. As he kissed her, his hand slid down her back and came to rest on the swell of her bottom. His tongue danced with hers and she returned the passion thrust for thrust.

The kiss went on a long time but he finally forced himself to stop and stare her in the eyes. "When we get these charges hanging over you dropped, I want to do that a whole lot more."

She smiled. "Me, too."

He let her go and stepped back. "If we're going to do

this, I better get out of here before I decide this is a better way to spend the evening."

"Good luck luring her out. I'll be waiting."

Win left and headed down the corridor to change into his dinner jacket and set their plan in motion.

ରେଡେ

Once Win left the compartment, Fiona removed her hat and straightened her hair from where he'd mussed it while they kissed. She smiled at the memory of his lips on hers. He really was a dream come true, but she worried a bit as well since she wasn't in the clear yet. What if his family didn't like him paying court to a lowly librarian of no consequence who was a murder suspect at this point in her life?

She shrugged her shoulders and, putting Win and his family firmly to the back of her mind, she moved around the small compartment, getting it ready for whatever was to come if Mrs. Perry took the bait and tried to come to do harm to her.

Fiona decided that she would wear the only pair of slacks she'd brought with her since it wouldn't be appropriate for her to actually wear her pajamas when Win or Mack was in her room. She giggled a bit at what her mum would think of her having men in her boudoir. She'd probably disown Fiona if she knew.

That thought brought out an involuntary snort. Being

disowned by one family member had already happened, when Fiona stood up to her father and moved out. It couldn't be helped, though. He'd become so overbearing and unstable that he scared her. He was the Nazi in the family and she hoped that information didn't come out—at least not while she was still on the train and under suspicion of murder.

A knock at the door interrupted her reverie. She opened the door to a waiter carrying a tray. He stepped inside and set the tray with the silver domed lid on the table. "Your dinner, madam. I hope it's to your satisfaction. The conductor asked your normal wait staff for suggestions for your meal and they chose for you."

Fiona took a deep breath and the scent of roasted beef of some sort with gravy wafted up to her nose. "It sure smells delightful. Thank you very much."

He bowed and backed out of the compartment. "I'll be back in a few moments with a bottle of wine and a glass. I hope the sommelier's choice will be suitable."

Fiona sat and before she could even lift the silver top, the waiter returned with the bottle. He poured a small amount for her to test and, once she nodded her acceptance, filled her glass. "*Bon appetit.* I will return in thirty minutes to collect the tray."

The moment the waiter cleared the door, Fiona inspected her dinner. She was correct. It was a lovely cut of beef bourguignon with diced carrots and potatoes. She inhaled again and almost passed out from the amazing aroma. She had no idea that she was so famished. She ate her meal in a hurry, and then moved away from the table to recline and enjoy her wine.

She propped her feet on the other end of the bench and let herself slump a little. Since Win was clearly on her side now, she allowed herself to relax and believe that everything would work out all right and that she would survive this crazy train trip.

Fiona enjoyed the quiet for a little while as she savored the taste of the wine. She soon realized she better stop drinking if she wanted her wits about her when her expected visitor came to call. It wouldn't do at all for Mrs. Perry to catch her drunk or impaired. It was imperative that she be alert.

# Chapter 15

Fear is, of all passions, that which weakens the judgment most. ~ *Cardinal de Retz, French Cardinal, 1613-1679*

After they finished their dinner, Win, Mack, and Cordelia moved from the dining car to the lounge. They sat at a table in the far corner and huddled over it so no one could overhear their conversation.

The waiter stepped over to take their drink orders. Mack and Win ordered brandy and Cordelia ordered a Pink Lady.

When the waiter brought the drinks, Mack nodded at Cordelia's. "Your brother said he drank whisky disguised

as tea during Prohibition and now you're drinking a cocktail that was invented to disguise bad gin back then.
What's the deal?"

"Since my friend Fiona is a big fan of gin, I wanted
to have a drink in her honor and this is the only way I can
abide gin." Cordelia took a sip and shuddered. "It's hide-
ous."

Mack glanced around the room. "Darn it, I don't see
Mrs. Perry in here. She never showed up in the dining
car, either. I wonder where she is."

"Maybe she's trying not to look suspicious. If she
waltzed in here to dinner after being widowed today, it
might not reflect nicely on her," Win said. "People might
talk."

"That's true. What if she doesn't show? Then what
will we do?" Cordelia asked.

Mack tapped the top of his glass with his index finger. "I've noticed that she seems to have made friends
with Lady Sarah Marchman. Maybe you could go over,
talk to the professor, and pull out the handkerchief. Hope-
fully, the word would then get back to Mrs. Perry."

"That's a good idea. I saw them come in ahead of us.
They took a table at the opposite end of the car. I'll go
over in a minute and see if that works." Win glanced
around the room. "We're running out of time. I don't
think the police will give in and not take Fiona to lock up
when we arrive in Istanbul. I know Ahmet and Faruk will
want to haul in their suspects if they can catch them. I

feel in my gut that the heroin issue is somehow related to the murders but I have no proof. All I know for certain is that I can't leave Fiona in a foreign country at the mercy of a system she doesn't understand and a language she doesn't speak."

Cordelia smiled at Win over the rim of her cocktail glass. "Big brother, I do believe you've fallen for my pal, Fi. Can it be true?"

"Interestingly enough, Cordelia, I think I have. It's odd, I know since I was so set against you making friends with her when we boarded, but it seemed that the more I saw her and talked to her the more I liked her."

Cordelia giggled. "Ahh. I get it. It was like constructing a building. Each meeting added a little more to the project?"

"A bit like that, I guess. I guess that's appropriate since I'm an engineer." Win laughed. "My feelings built as I continued to encounter Fiona. At first, I didn't think much of her since she was so quiet and subdued. Her strength as she's gone through this ordeal has really impressed me."

"It's impressed me, too, mate." Mack drained his glass. "Go on over and have that chat with the Marchmans so we can get this production underway. Like you said, we're quickly running out of time as well as train track."

"All right. Keep an eye out and signal me if you see Abigail Perry come in." Win stood and picked up his glass. "Once I lay the groundwork, then we can stake out Fiona's compartment."

"I like that plan. Until then, I'll enjoy the lovely Cordelia's company."

"Please don't blow my cover as her husband. I need to keep that intact at least until we debark. No hand-holding or canoodling." Win glanced over at his sister. "Can you manage to behave for one more evening? If I promise to let you run wild in Istanbul?"

"Very funny, Barry," Cordelia said, "as if you'd ever let me run wild even in our hometown of New Haven much less in a foreign country."

"Please try. I need you to behave."

"I'll make sure she does." Mack stood as well. "Come, Cordelia. I think we need a refill and maybe a change of seat so we can keep an eye on the whole room at once." He held his hand out to her and assisted her to her feet.

Win approached the table where the Oxford don sat with his wife, Lady Sarah, and Jacques Cassel. Cassel was chomping on his ever-present mints even as he drank what appeared to be whisky. Win shuddered again at the thought of how those two things would taste together.

"Come and join us, Barrington. We're almost to Istanbul. Time to celebrate the end of the journey. We're determined to drink ourselves under the table. I have to give a lecture tomorrow night but that's way in the future, isn't it?"

Win pulled up a chair and sat. "What about hangovers, sir?"

"Hangovers be damned, boy." Hugo laughed and then called out to the bartender, "Bring another round for me and my friends."

Win wondered how he was going to broach the serious subject of the murders with Marchman being so boisterous.

It seemed as if the man were almost demented with the need to drink.

Before Win could give it much thought, Cassel said, "I heard they have that little librarian under some kind of house arrest in her compartment. Did you know that?"

Thankful that the man brought it up, Win nodded. "I *did* hear that. Can you even imagine her doing something like that? She seems a bit too meek for using a knife. A person has to get pretty close to kill with a knife, don't they?"

Cassel shook his head as if to illustrate his disbelief. "You're right on both counts. I can't fathom a little girl like that who probably hides behind the stacks in the library if someone sneezes too loud as a cold-blooded killer."

"Don't be fooled, gentlemen, the quiet ones are always the sneaky ones," Lady Sarah said. "What better person to be a spy as poor Donald Perry thought she was, than one who people overlook when she's in the room?

She can stand among a crowd and listen to private conversations and no one even notices she's standing there,"

"You may be right there, dear." Hugo patted his
wife's hand. "I still somehow don't want her to be guilty.
She seems so sweet and we had a lovely conversation
about how nervous she was to make her speech about the
train's history."

Sensing it was the perfect time to bring out the handkerchief, Win pulled it from his pocket. "Let me show
you something."

The other three at the table leaned forward. "What's
that, Barrington?" Hugo asked.

"It's a handkerchief that may belong to the person
who killed Mr. Perry. I asked Miss Vancleave about it but
she denied it was hers." Win stretched it out and ran his
fingers over the lace at the edges. "This looks pretty
unique. Almost as if it were special ordered. Have any of
you seen anyone else on the train with a handkerchief like
this one?"

"Not to be unkind, Mr. Barrington but I'd think Miss
Vancleave couldn't afford something like this on a librarian's salary. If she were a Nazi spy well placed in the
United Kingdom, though, I bet she'd be well paid and
could buy them by the dozen. I wouldn't discount the fact
that she said it wasn't hers."

Lady Sarah's voice grated on Win's nerves. She sure
sounded like a snob now. It was a change from her normal tone. He didn't like it.

"But you don't recognize it? You haven't seen another woman on board with one like it?" Win asked.

Lady Sarah took it from Win, rubbed the lace edge with her index finger and then ran the palm of her hand over the center. "Can't say that I have." She passed it to Cassel. "What about you, Jacques? Does it look familiar to you?"

Cassel wiped his hands on the napkin on the table before he took the hanky. "No. I can't say that I have."

"So, neither of you have seen Mrs. Perry with one like this?" Win asked.

"Mrs. Perry?" Lady Sarah shook her head. "Indeed not. I've been around the poor dear a lot on this trip and I can't say that I've seen her with one like this."

Win couldn't figure out why Lady Sarah would lie about the hanky. He had a moment of doubt about Fiona's statement, that she'd seen Abigail Perry with the exact handkerchief but shook it off. He could either choose to believe the woman he cared so much about or not. He couldn't keep doubting her.

Hugo leaned across the table and took the piece of cloth from Cassel. "Let me see that."

Once Hugo had it in his hand, Win asked, "What about you, sir. Have you seen anyone on board with such an item?"

"I actually have. I think it *does* belong to Mrs. Perry." Hugo stared at Win. "Where did you say you got this?"

"I didn't say. Are you sure it belongs to Mrs. Perry?"

"I can't be positive but it seems as if we had a conversation one evening when Mr. Perry was there. He was bragging about his empire of woolens. He also said he could afford to have his wife's lace hand made for her and that the design was an exclusive. He showed us some of it and this looks like it." Hugo turned to his wife. "Don't you remember, dearest?"

"I remember the conversation dear but I don't think this was the lace pattern." Lady Sarah stood. "But speaking of sweet Mrs. Perry, I really should check on the poor thing. She's been in her compartment grieving all day."

Hugo reached out and squeezed his wife's hand. "Yes, love, you should. Go on now and we'll be here drinking the night away. I'll see you later. Don't wait up,"

Lady Sarah turned toward the door. As she walked out, she turned back and blew her husband a kiss.

As soon as she was gone, Hugo pulled out his pipe. "Thanks for reminding my wife that she had a friend to call on. She's not the biggest fan of my pipe tobacco and I actually think she took some of mine and threw it off the train."

"What makes you think that?" Cassel asked.

Hugo took a pinch of the tobacco and placed it in the bowl of the pipe. "I asked her to hold my pouch for me and the next time I asked her for it, she couldn't find it anywhere. I think it was an act. I truly believe she hurled it off and into the countryside."

Win's gut clenched as he got a whiff of it. He reached over and held his hand out. "May I?"

"I didn't think you were much of a smoker, Barrington." Hugo grinned. "You're welcome to share. It's my own blend. I'm kind of picky about my tobacco like Donald Perry was about his wife's lace."

Taking the proffered tobacco, Win placed it up to his nose but he already knew. It was the same as what he found in the coat pocket. His blood froze in his veins and it took a few seconds for his legs to get the message from his brain. Fiona was in danger. He needed to get to her—and now.

Lurching to his feet and knocking the chair over in the process, Win stepped away from the table, tossing the packet to the floor in his haste.

As he darted toward the door, he called over to Mack. "Hurry. Let's go."

# Chapter 16

*In skating over thin ice, our safety is in our speed. ~ Ralph Waldo Emerson, American Writer, 1803-1882*

Fiona was ready for the fight. Or at least she told herself that she was. The nervousness that had crept back in after her rest, forced her to pace around the small space in an effort to calm down. It seemed like ages since the waiter came for her empty tray but she knew it really hadn't been all that long. Every minute seemed to stretch into an hour.

She wondered what kind of progress Win was making with Mrs. Perry. She wished she could leave the compartment and, for the first time in her life, appreciated the people who she'd heard of who had experienced cabin fever. It was quite vexing to be behind a door and not allowed to open it and walk free. How she would handle a real prison preyed on her mind.

Trying to find something to do, she spent a little time clearing up the area in the small closet/sink area so Mack or Win could fit in there when they came to hide and get ready for the setup of Mrs. Perry. "I wish they would come on," Fiona muttered under her breath after taking yet another turn around the room. It was getting tedious waiting for someone else's timetable.

Idly wishing the waiter had left the bottle of wine but knowing that it wouldn't be good to have finished it off since she needed her senses about her, she finally flopped down on the bench seat and tried to read the *Tatler* magazine she'd brought along on the trip with her.

Fiona flipped through the pages. It was no good. She couldn't concentrate. She tossed it to the floor and rose from the bench. She walked over to the window and placed her head on the cool plate glass. It was pitch dark outside but she could see some lights in the distance. Her heart lurched as those lights reminded her that the train would soon be arriving in the city and the Istanbul station. Her skin itched and she knew how a snake must feel as it shed its skin.

Tired of the house arrest and stressed out by the long wait, Fiona turned to the door. She stared at it for a few moments and decided she was going to leave the compartment before she went completely insane. If they hauled her to jail or tied her up in another area of the train, so be it.

No matter the cost, she needed a few minutes of freedom.

Fiona turned the handle and flung the door open.

Lady Sarah Marchman stood there with her fist raised as if she were in the process of knocking. Fiona let out a gasp. "Oh my, you scared me. Come on in. I'm glad for the company. I was just going a little stir crazy."

"I can only imagine. I heard you were confined by the police until we get to Istanbul and wanted to come by and see if you needed anything." Lady Sarah held out a small box. "I happened to have these chocolates in my pocket. I thought you might enjoy a taste."

Fiona showed her in and indicated the bench on the right side of the compartment.

She let out a bitter laugh as she took the seat opposite Lady Sarah. "Have a seat. I'd love a tiny piece of chocolate. The conductor was nice enough to bring me some dinner and wine but they didn't send dessert. Maybe they think I need to be punished."

"Nonsense. Everyone on the train likes you and I don't think anyone wishes you were in this situation."

"Thank you. I appreciate that." Fiona reached over to the proffered box and took a dark chocolate from its spot. She took a bite and sighed. It was raspberry filled. Her favorite.

Lady Sarah watched Fiona as she chewed. Once the chocolate was gone, Fiona said, "That was divine. Aren't you going to have any?"

Lady Sarah replaced the lid on the box. "No. I don't think so."

"I can't believe you don't like chocolate."

"I didn't say I don't like it. I merely stated that I wasn't going to have any of *this* chocolate."

Fiona had a hard time focusing on Lady Sarah's face. Maybe she had too much wine after all? She opened her mouth to speak and the words came out as if in slow motion. "Why did you say *this* chocolate like that?"

"That's easy my dear. This particular chocolate has been spiked with a very strong narcotic."

"Excuse me?" Fiona slurred the words.

"I sometimes find it easier to kill someone who I've grown to like if I can ease them into a coma-like state first so they don't fight me." Lady Sarah pushed the hair that had fallen onto her forehead out of her eyes. "It distresses me to have to get physical in my work. I much prefer an easy, impersonal hit where I don't have a connection to the mark. It's really a difficult thing to do, you know—killing someone you like."

"Why do it then?"

"It's my job dear. After all, I took the fee, so I need to clean up my mess."

"Wait. Someone paid you to *kill* me?" Fiona tried to sit up but found that the spike of adrenaline that the woman's words brought out failed her and she slumped over, her head on the bench.

"No. You weren't the intended target but unfortunately, you got in the way and now I must eliminate you like I had to neutralize Lucien after he discovered my plans."

Fiona could barely hold her eyes open but she struggled to understand all that Lady Sarah was saying in case she lived through this ordeal and could tell someone. "You killed Lucien?"

"Sadly, yes. I really must be losing my touch. I've had way too much collateral damage in this operation. Poor Lucien, then Abigail—although I admit that was my fault for thinking to get her involved—and now you." Sarah glanced at her watch. "Much as I'm enjoying our chat dear, I must finish this and go before someone comes along and finds me here with you."

Fiona closed her eyes. She was so tired all she wanted to do was sleep. She sensed the seat of the bench sink down as if someone sat next to her. With effort, Fiona lifted one eyelid to peer out. Her limbs were so numb and her brain so fogged, she couldn't even muster the energy to fight against the knife Sarah Marchman held to her neck.

"I really am sorry you have to go like this. I did quite like you, you know."

The compartment door slammed open.

"Stop right now."

Win's voice carried across the space and was the last thing Fiona heard before she passed out from the drug in the chocolate.

ఞ౩ఞ౩

Win's heart almost stopped beating when he opened the door to the sight of Lady Sarah with Fiona draped in her lap and a knife at her throat. "Get away from her. Right now."

"Oh, I don't think so, Mr. Barrington. The moment I move away from her is the moment you grab me and turn me over to the police. I think not. We will be pulling in to Istanbul soon and Miss Vancleave will be my ticket off this train."

"You can't possibly believe that you can get away with killing Mr. Perry and walk off this train with no one in pursuit. You're well and caught, ma'am," Mack said from behind Win's shoulder.

"If that's true, I have nothing to lose by killing her right now, do I?"

The woman's smile made Win nervous. There was no doubt about it. She was a stone-cold killer. All the things he'd learned about the person he was pursuing on this trip ran through his head at once and it dawned on him that this lady—a true lady, the daughter of a peer of the realm—was the one he sought. The one who's code-name was Senior Assassin.

He wanted to yell and scream his frustration. He'd succeeded in finding the person he sought when he left Paris but at what cost? Was he going to lose Fiona in this quest? How did he not see it before? He couldn't believe that he'd been so fooled by this woman. She carried her title with grace and dignity and he never looked past the façade. He deserved to be fired.

"It would be extremely foolish of you to kill her now because my friend and I would immediately kill you as well." Win hoped his logic worked.

"Looks like we're at a stalemate then." Lady Sarah shrugged. "What do you think we should do?"

"Why'd you kill Perry? Was that why you were on this train? To assassinate him? What's he into that you'd be hired to off him?" Win asked.

He could tell Mack was doing something behind him but didn't want to turn around to see what. He needed to keep Sarah's attention focused on him while his brain ran different scenarios through his head. It wouldn't do for her to focus on Mack in case Mack had another plan to stop her that he was going to implement.

"What makes you think I was hired to do anything?" she sneered.

"You're *Senior Assassin*, aren't you?"

Sarah inclined her head. "Bravo, Mr. Barrington. What do you know about Senior Assassin anyway? Aren't you some industrialist from Connecticut? Weapons manufacturer? Or is it toys?"

"I know a lot about you, lady, and I'm going to be the one who stops you from killing anyone else."

"Oh, I doubt that, dear boy."

Win wanted to wipe the smirk off the woman's face as she called him *dear boy*. "Just because you've been killing for more years than I've been alive doesn't mean that I can't be the one to end your spree." He wondered if Mack was getting help or if he'd drawn his weapon. They needed to end this standoff before Fiona got hurt.

"You need to go now, Mr. Barrington. I can see the lights of the city and I'm either getting off this train in a few moments with Miss Vancleave as my hostage or she's going to be dead." Lady Sarah peered down at Fiona. "Unless she is already. If I gave her too much."

Win took a couple of steps into the room, thinking Lady Sarah was distracted.

The woman whipped her head back around. Her smile had grown bigger. Win was confused for a moment until he saw the gun she had pointed at his chest. Where had that come from?

"I wonder exactly who you are, young man. You have some idea about who I might be but you've obviously not been trained well, as I keep surprising you."

"Maybe I have a surprise for you that I'm waiting to pull until you're complacent. You know, that moment when you underestimate me."

She threw her head back and laughed. He took the chance he'd been waiting for. Leaping across the compartment, Win threw himself at Lady Sarah. He snatched her wrist that held the gun and broke it. He heard the bone snap as he kicked the weapon away.

She cried out but grabbed the knife she'd placed next to her on the bench and, with her good hand, sliced the air toward Win. When Lady Sarah moved, Fiona fell to the floor and landed with a thud.

Lady Sarah brandished the knife and moved closer to Win.

"That's enough," Mack yelled.

Win glanced over at Mack. He had his own firearm pointed at Lady Sarah. "It's all over, lady. I don't have any idea what you and my friend were talking about, but it's clear to me that you're someone that we need to haul in to the authorities. I happen to have signaled the steward for this section to go and get the Turkish police on board so they can take you into custody."

"The United States War Department and British SIS will probably want to get their hands on her pretty quick," Win explained. "She's a contract killer who has been on their most wanted list for a very long time."

"We're lucky we got her then," Mack said. "See if you can restrain her until Ahmet gets here."

Win stepped toward Lady Sarah who had gone surprising quiet. Before he could touch her, she ran toward the window and threw herself against it as if to try to escape from the train. The window didn't break and her body ricocheted off the paneling and glass. She landed on her bottom just as the two Turkish officers entered the room followed by the head conductor and the steward.

The officers took control and escorted Lady Sarah out of the compartment.

As soon as they were gone, Win knelt down to feel Fiona's pulse, placing his first two fingers on her carotid artery. Relieved that she was still breathing, he scooped her into his arms.

"What are you going to do now, mate? I think you need to be in on the questioning of Lady Sarah." Mack held his arms out. "Let me take her to Cordelia and we'll take care of her."

"There will be time to hear from Lady Sarah. Right now, I need to be sure Fiona is all right." Win strode out of the cabin with Fiona still in his arms and Mack trailing behind.

# Chapter 17

Justice is truth in action. ~ *Benjamin Disraeli, British Statesman, 1804-1881*

There wasn't time to interrogate Lady Sarah later, after all. When they had her isolated for questioning, she asked for a glass of water. One of the officers unlocked her handcuffs and handed her a cup.

Before anyone could stop her, she popped a cyanide pill, crushed it between her teeth, and killed herself. It only took a few minutes for her to die and they didn't get any information from her.

Upon a search of the train for Mrs. Perry, they found her tied up in her own compartment. She'd been beaten and could barely speak but Win insisted on questioning her for his report.

The train pulled into the station. As the other passengers debarked, Win sat in the library with the two Turkish policemen and some local officers as they took Mrs. Perry's statement. They let him take the lead since he was the one who needed to make his report to his superiors about the death of Senior Assassin. It wasn't clear at the moment if any criminal charges would be brought against Mrs. Perry.

She sat in a wingback chair and her facial expressions ran the gamut from terrified to smug. Win couldn't decide at first whether the woman was an innocent victim or a part of a conspiracy. As the questioning went on, it became clear exactly how involved she was.

"I don't know why Lady Sarah thought I would go along with her plan to seduce that odious Johnny Rozzelle but she approached me about doing so after the first night in the lounge. I think she could probably tell my marriage wasn't the greatest. My husband constantly belittled me and maybe Lady Sarah thought I could use a man to pay attention to me. In fact, she said he told her that he thought I was attractive and wanted to spend time with me." Abigail shook her head. "Turns out, that wasn't true but by the time I found that out, I was already in too deep."

"What do you mean?" Win asked.

Abigail sniffed and wiped her nose with the back of

her hand. "I was involved with him sexually. It seems that even though he didn't tell her that he was interested in me, once I made the first move, he was perfectly happy to take me to his bed."

"Did Lady Sarah ever tell you why she needed you for that purpose?"

"Not in so many words. She said she had a job to do that related to his drug trade. I had no idea he was a drug supplier when I met him but Sarah told me he was. She said he had a lot of heroin he was smuggling and that she needed someone to get close to him. She said she couldn't do it because she was a police investigator and he may have seen her before."

Win raised his eyebrows. "And you believed her? A daughter of an English peer married to an Oxford don tells you she's a copper and you *believe* her?"

"What better way to be an investigator? Someone who has access to the higher classes would be the perfect person to be secretly on the payroll of the constabulary, wouldn't they? In fact, when I got involved with Rozzelle, he showed me his cache of drugs in the back, so of course I believed her. What she said was true, after all."

When Mrs. Perry put it that way, it did kind of make sense and, besides, Lady Sarah's family background *had* provided her with the perfect cover to assassinate people, especially when she got to travel with her lecturing husband. "Once you established the relationship with Rozzelle and saw the drugs, what happened next?"

"Lady Sarah said I needed to tell him I'd help him so I agreed to assist in smuggling heroin in some of my husband's wool shipments." She leaned forward. "This is how your Cordelia got tossed off the train."

"How so?"

"We were in the back of the train and I'd brought Lady Sarah along so she could see the drugs. I was thinking she would arrest Rozzelle but she didn't. She started chatting with him and his entourage. Your wife came up about then and Rozzelle panicked. He threw her off."

Win nodded at two of the Turkish police as they left the library. He knew they were going to try to stop Rozzelle from getting off the train if it wasn't already too late. They had him on several charges based on what Mrs. Perry had stated.

They had her, too but he wasn't going to enlighten her about that just yet.

"What about all the mint wrappers we kept finding? Did Jacques Cassel have anything to do with any of this?" Win asked.

"No." Abigail laughed a little hysterically. "It was perfect, wasn't it? That Frenchman kept leaving those all over the place. He thought the waiters would clean up behind him. Lady Sarah suggested that we put them in our pockets and strew them around the area in the back of the train in case anyone got suspicious. They would think Cassel was involved. In fact, that's how that nosy steward Lucien got killed."

"How's that?" Win held back his smile. They were going to solve all these crimes right now, here in the station.

"The steward came upon Lady Sarah dressed in her black cape with the hood. She wasn't sure he saw her face clearly, but she was dropping some wrappers on the floor and he asked too many questions. She told me she had to shut him up before he told what he saw or figured out it was her. I think he even saw some of the blocks of heroin but I'm not sure about that part."

"What happened after that? How did your husband get killed?"

"I don't know for sure but I think Lady Sarah did it. Donald heard us talking about Rozzelle and the drugs and hit the ceiling. He was furious and threatened to divorce me. The next thing I knew, he was dead."

Win was sure that the lady was lying. Of course, she knew who killed her husband. It had to be either her or Lady Sarah. He was sure Abigail was pretending to be confused since she hadn't been told that her co-conspirator was dead. "How did it happen that Miss Vancleave's papers were in your husband's hands?"

"Since he thought she was a Nazi because her name is German and was blabbing that all over the train, Lady Sarah said it would be perfect if we framed the librarian for his death."

"So you *did* know that Lady Sarah killed your husband and you knew it before she did it."

Abigail frowned. "I didn't say that."

Win laughed. "Sure you did."

The woman either thought he was gullible or stupid and he was neither.

He loved it when they walked right in to a confession without even realizing it. This lady wasn't going to make it out of Europe any time soon.

She crossed her arms over her chest in a protective gesture. "You can't prove any of this. Lady Sarah and Johnny Rozzelle are too savvy to talk to you so I'm not going to say another word either."

Win debated whether to tell Mrs. Perry that Lady Sarah was dead but decided that the Istanbul police might not want that information out yet so he kept quiet and stood. He glanced over at Ahmet. "She's all yours. I have what I need as soon as the stenographer types it." He turned to the typist. "I'll be back here at the station on Tuesday to take the train back to Paris. Do you think you can have this ready by then?"

"No problem. I'll be here with it by the scheduled departure time," the man replied as he handed his business card to Win.

"Thank you." Win shook hands all around. "Please excuse me. I have somewhere I need to be." He turned and left the train, hoping Cordelia had gotten the luggage to their hotel with the assistance of one of the porters. She'd insisted on going on without him as she wanted to be in a room that didn't move for a while.

෴

Relieved finally to be off the train and nursing a bit of a hangover from whatever Lady Sarah had spiked the candy with, Fiona turned down Cordelia's offer of a lift to the hotel where she and Win were staying. Fiona had her own room reserved at the Excelsior Hotel and couldn't wait to get there and unwind. Her speech would be taking place that very evening and she wanted some time to get her thoughts in order and recreate the notes stolen from her compartment.

She'd given her statement of what happened with Lady Sarah to the Turkish authorities before she debarked but they hadn't given her many details about the investigation. They wouldn't let her talk to Mack or Win because they said they wanted unbiased testimony from all three of them.

She really thought, though, that Win would try to see her before she debarked and she turned down Cordelia's offer for that reason, too. When he didn't come, she became a little despondent but realized that perhaps he regretted the kiss and really had no interest in continuing a relationship. It wouldn't be appropriate to keep up the acquaintance if he didn't want her, so she finally gave up and left the train. She knew she would treasure his kisses always and that they would be something to relive over and over again when she returned to Worchester.

Arriving in a taxi at her hotel, she checked in and

took a leisurely bath complete with bubbles and really hot water. The train was nice but the facilities for cleanliness were lacking in quality and luxury.

Once she was clean and dry, Fiona dressed in her robe and called for room service. She decided to have a sandwich at her desk as she worked on the presentation for that evening. It wasn't too hard to recreate the notes she'd lost since she had immersed herself in the train lore at the library for weeks.

Before Fiona knew it, it was time to get ready for the lecture. She wore an ivory linen suit with a white button-front blouse, silk stockings and a pair of beige shoes. She placed her cream-colored hat on her head, pulled on her gloves and picked up her briefcase.

The man at the front desk had arranged for a taxi to take her to the institute and she arrived at the door to the hotel right on time to meet it.

Upon arrival at her destination, Fiona stepped out of the car and ran almost straight into Hugo Marchman. Her gut clenched and she backed up in horror.

"I'm so sorry, my dear. I didn't mean to startle you." Hugo smiled and held his hand out. "Please forgive me."

Since he wasn't in jail, Fiona presumed he'd been found not to have anything to do with his wife's behavior but she needed to ask anyway. "Did you speak to the police about your wife?"

"Ah, yes, I did. You have nothing to fear from me." The don took her by the elbow and led her toward the entrance to the building. "I had no idea what my bride had been doing all these years. I thought it quite odd that she never seemed to tire of traveling with me to these lectures and was always interested in where I was going to accept engagements. Most of the other gents' wives got tired of it after a year or two of marriage."

"You really had no idea? What about the money? How did she explain the money she was making?"

"Well, you know, there was her trust fund. Her great-great grandfather—I can't recall how many greats back—set up a fund for all of the females in his line so that they would have ready money for themselves and not have to rely on a husband for an allowance. I'm afraid I assumed that the investment that the man made was doing well. I never asked any questions as she used those funds as she saw fit. My salary and my fees for speaking engagements paid our regular living expenses."

Fiona stepped aside as Mr. Marchman opened the door. "I find it so shocking that she was an international assassin."

"After you." He bowed. As Fiona stepped past him, he added, "You can't have been more shocked than I, my dear. After all, I've been married to her almost thirty-five years. It was quite a blow, I must say."

"I'm really sorry."

"Ah, no need. No need. I'll move past it."

"Why are you here, anyway? Shouldn't you be planning how to get her body home and buried?"

"There's plenty of time for that. The train doesn't leave until Tuesday and I'll return on it." Marchman winked. "Besides, I hear there's a lovely librarian from the English countryside who's presenting a talk on the Orient Express here today. I couldn't very well miss that, could I?"

"I'm glad you came. It'll be nice to see a friendly face in the crowd."

"I'm sure you'll do fine. Look." Hugo pointed to three men who approached. "It seems the welcoming committee is here. I'll head inside and get a good seat." He kissed her lightly on the cheek. "As they say in the theatre, 'Break a leg'."

She waved at his retreating back and then strode toward the men who were closing in on her. Fiona held out her hand when they reached her and introduced herself.

After the greetings and introductions, one of the men led her backstage and gave her some last minute instructions. Fiona approached the podium and set her notes on the slanted top.

Wiping her sweaty hands on her skirt and hoping they weren't going to leave marks on the light material, she watched as the curtains slid apart at the middle exposing her to the audience. When the curtain was fully open, Fiona looked out at the crowd, amazed to see how large it was. She could scarcely believe that this many people would turn out to see a lowly librarian from the countryside of England as Hugo Marchman had stated.

Thinking of Hugo reminded her that there would be one friendly face out there and she sought him with her eyes. She glanced from row to row and stopped in shock when she found him seated on the third one right in the center. Beside him sat Winchester Barrington, IV.

Her knees buckled for a second as she looked out on Win's handsome face. He gave her a small wave and winked at her.

She found strength in his support and started her presentation with her voice strong and competent.

# Chapter 18

It is a truth, universally acknowledged, that a single man in possession of a good fortune must be in want of a wife. ~ *Jane Austen, English Novelist, 1775-1817*

Before Fiona knew it, the presentation was over and people surrounded her, congratulating her for the fine presentation. It seemed she'd done more than a passable job and she was ecstatic by all the plaudits and praise. They invited her to return any time to speak again. All the accolades gave her ego a much-needed boost.

When the crowd finally cleared, Fiona found herself staring at Win as he stood beside Hugo. Hugo was the first to move and enveloped her in a hug. "Well done, my dear. You have the makings of a great lecturer and I'd be honored to have you at Oxford in any of my classes or tutorials."

"Thank you. You have no idea how much that means to me. For a don to think such good things about me is very special."

"Speaking of good things and very special, I think there's someone here who wants to spend time with you and I'm going to get out of the way and let that happen." Marchman bowed. "I hope to see you on the train on the return journey."

Hugo walked away and Win stepped forward. "You left before I could say goodbye."

"Cordelia said you were busy questioning Mrs. Perry and I wasn't sure how long it would take." She didn't tell him how long she'd waited, hoping that he would show up. "I needed to have some peace before this presentation but you could've come to the hotel to speak to me. I told Cordelia where I was staying."

"I didn't see her when I arrived at our suite. She left a note that she and Plant were out visiting some of the mosques. It seems my sister has a penchant for onion domes." He laughed and shrugged. "Who knew?"

"I had no idea either. It doesn't quite seem to be something Cordelia would enjoy. I tend to think that Mack wanted to see them and that Cordelia wanted to see Mack."

"Enough about that sister of mine who can drive a teetotaler to alcoholism. What do you say if I take you to dinner? To celebrate your grand success." Win swung his arm out to encompass the room.

"Sounds divine. I'm famished. I only had a sandwich all day. What's good in Istanbul?" Fiona dared to hope that Win was here for more than dinner. Would he declare that he wanted to see her again? Or would he tell her he was going back to America as soon as he could since he'd caught the assassin he sought?

"There's tava which is a kind of stew or if you like dumplings, there's manti and there's always the standby of kebabs." Win reached for her briefcase. "Let me carry that."

She handed him the case. "Thanks. I appreciate it and I think I'd like to try the tava."

"I know the perfect place. Let's go."

She followed him outside where he hailed a cab that took them to a small restaurant tucked into a side street not far from the train station.

Fiona could see the roof of that building as the cab took a turn down what almost appeared to be a wide alleyway rather than a real road.

The sign above the door said *Beyti*. They stepped inside and Fiona let out a tiny gasp. The place was lovely. The interior was magical with red gossamer wall hangings as well as ruby red velvet upholstery on the chairs. The tablecloths were a golden shade and the mahogany wood of all the furniture seemed to glow in the low lighting of the room.

Win got them a table and, once seated, Fiona smiled across at him. "Even if the food is terrible, I'm loving this place. It's so very Turkish. I think it's almost from a book."

Win reached over and took hold of Fiona's right hand. "I'm going to enjoy this meal even if the food is bad as well because seeing your eyes shine with pleasure makes me happier than I ever thought possible."

His words made her heart melt. From a man who'd been so forbidding when first encountered these words had to have huge import, didn't they? She knew her cheeks flushed since it seemed so hot inside her own body. Luckily, the waiter brought them each a glass of water at that moment. Fiona grabbed hers as if she were on fire and needed the brigade to put her out. She gulped down the liquid so fast she choked.

Win raced around the table to pat her on the back. "Are you all right?"

Fiona nodded and managed to gasp out the words, "Sorry. That went down wrong."

Win peered down at her. "Are you sure you're fine?"

"Yes. Sit. Let's order. We're the center of attention."

Win retook his seat. He spoke to the waiter who still hovered and ordered for them both. Once they were alone again, Win grinned. "I think I know what really happened."

"Between Abigail Perry and Lady Sarah?"

"No, silly. When you choked a few minutes ago."

"I told you. The water went down wrong."

"You grabbed that glass as if it was a life raft and you just fell off the Titanic. I think you gulped the water too fast because you were embarrassed about what I said and you didn't know how to reply."

"Wow. You think so? Why would I be embarrassed? You didn't say anything inappropriate. In fact, I can scarcely recall what you said at all," Fiona lied.

"You forget I'm a trained interrogator, Miss Vancleave. Do you care to hazard a guess as to why I know you're lying about that statement you just made about your recall of the conversation?"

"Oh good grief. I'm not lying."

"There it goes again."

She crossed her arms. "What?"

"The delightful way your facial flush travels down your neck and to your cleavage when you're fibbing."

Before she could respond, their food was delivered. Fiona snatched her spoon and dipped it into her stew. Maybe the infernal man would stop talking if she got involved in eating and chewing. Surely he would hush if he had his mouth full. Wouldn't he?

She took three bites before she realized he was still staring at her. She swallowed and glanced up. The look in his eyes took her breath away. She'd never had anyone eye her in the way he was—as if he adored her.

"What's wrong, Fiona?" His words were a whisper only for her to hear.

"Nothing." She pointed her spoon at his food. "Eat. Stop gaping at me and eat your food."

"What is food when there is such beauty before me?"

"Oh, stop. Now you're being nonsensical." Fiona turned her attention back to her food. If the insufferable man wasn't going to eat, that was his problem. She was enjoying the flavor of the stew and meat and was determined to finish her meal even if she had to dine with an audience.

After a few moments, from the corner of her eye, she saw him pick up his own spoon and dig in. Good. Now she could eat in peace and hope not to spill anything on her light-colored clothes.

Eventually, she had to look up at him. Her food was gone and now it was time to face her companion and try to have a normal conversation. She smiled as he tucked his napkin under the side of his dish.

"Are you full? Do you want dessert?" Win asked.

"No. I think I've had enough." She wiped her mouth. "I probably should get back to my hotel."

Win tossed some bills on the table to pay the tab that the waiter had already delivered. "The night is barely begun. How about going for a stroll?"

"Sure. I guess I should walk off some of that rich food."

He came around to her side of the table, pulled out

her chair, and assisted her to her feet. Taking her by the elbow, he led her out to the street, hailed a taxi, and instructed the driver to take them to the Grove area.

They stopped at the corner and Win led Fiona over to a walking path alongside the Bosphorus. He tucked her arm in his and they ambled down the path. "This is some of the best views you can see in Istanbul," he said.

"It is beautiful. What a lovely country this is. I'd love to spend some time exploring it."

"Then let's plan on it. We can tour tomorrow. I have to be on the train back to Paris on Tuesday and I imagine you're going back then as well."

"I am. I wish I could get home some other way as I really don't relish another train ride so soon after my house arrest."

"I won't let that happen again."

Fiona tried to laugh off her fear but wasn't successful. "How can you help it? That train is a virtual moving crime machine. I'm quite terrified to get on it again."

Win led her over to a bench and pulled her down beside him. "I want us to share a compartment on the way back to Paris."

"*What*? Are you crazy? You want to have two fake wives with you on the train now? What a scandal, sir."

Win smiled then lightly kissed her on the lips. "No. I don't want two fake wives, Fiona Vancleave."

"Well it's most improper anyway for you to share a compartment with me. Even if your sister is along."

"But it's not improper for a bride to share a compartment with her groom, is it?"

"Of course not, but that's the point, isn't it? We're not married."

Win tutted and shook his head as if in sadness. "For the moment, that *is* true."

Her heart seized. What was he saying? Was he joking? Toying with her? She stared up at his face. He wasn't giving anything away with his stoic look. Confused, she looked down at her hands as she twisted them together.

His large palm covered her fists and she sensed more than saw him move off the bench and onto one knee.

She dared to raise her eyes to meet his. Love shone from his face as he stared at her. "Fiona Vancleave, I find that I'm unable to continue to live my life without you in it. My career is a dangerous one, and I'm afraid with the situation in Europe changing every day that it will only get more and more perilous. I know it's unfair of me to ask you to be my wife, when the world seems to be at a point of imploding, but I can't help myself. I love you beyond all measure and I must ask."

Fiona removed her hands from his grasp and raised them to her mouth. She could hardly believe it. This man—this handsome, worldly, wealthy, savvy man wanted *her*. He wanted her to be by his side as his companion, his wife? She shook her head.

Disappointment ravaged his face.

She held out her hand and touched his right cheek. Tears streamed down her face. "Don't. I'm not saying no. I'm shaking my head in disbelief. What do you see in me? With all the women you've met and been around, why me? I don't understand what I have that makes you want me above all others."

"That right there is part of it, Fiona. You're so wonderful and amazing and you don't even realize it. You're one of those ladies that any man would kill to have for a wife and I want you. More than my own life, I want you and you alone."

"I don't think I'll ever understand it but I'm thrilled that you think I'm that special and I don't care what kind of jeopardy I may face. I confess, I want you as well."

Win let out a whoop of joy then scooped Fiona off the bench and into his arms. He covered her face with kisses eventually capturing her mouth with his. His tongue delighted her as it invaded her mouth and danced with hers.

When he finally let her up for air, he grinned. "Was there a *yes* in there somewhere?"

She smiled. "Absolutely, positively, completely, a yes."

"Then let's get off my knees. I'm dying here." He stood and assisted her to her feet.

"Don't die yet. We have to find a preacher, my love."

Win hugged her close. "Maybe Cordelia, my former

wife, found one today on her visits to all the churches and mosques of Istanbul."

"Let's hope so. I don't care if it's an imam or a priest or a plain old vicar who performs the ceremony. I want to return home as Mrs. Winchester Barrington, IV."

Win waggled his brows at his bride-to-be. "And I want to get to work on creating Master Winchester Barrington, V."

"Wait just a second." She held her hand up. "I have one caveat to this proposal about having children."

"What's that, my darling? Anything. I'll agree to anything."

"No daughter of mine will be named Winnie Fred. You *must* promise me that, Win."

Win winked and hugged her close. "Oh, no, my dear, I can't promise such a thing as that. You ask way too much of me."

She laughed and pushed on his chest as if to escape his embrace. "I can't marry you then."

"You drive a hard bargain, Miss Vancleave, but for you, I'll make the sacrifice. I solemnly swear that if we're blessed with a baby girl, I shall not name her Winnie Fred. She will be named—" He paused with his index finger on his chin as if thinking, then his eyes lit up with amusement. "—Winchessie, after her father, of course."

Fiona merely giggled.


THE END

## About the Author

Sherry Fowler Chancellor is a practicing attorney who lives on the beautiful Gulf Coast of Florida. When she's not working on behalf of her clients, she's busy penning a new story or hanging out with her friends and family in their own little slice of paradise. Her novel, Senior Assassin, is due to be released by Black Opal Books in late 2014.